INITIATION NIGHT

Samantha crouched low and moved fast, covering the space to the window in twenty steps. She stayed slightly hunkered beneath it as she worked up her courage to look in.

Slowly, slowly, she rose, leg muscles tight and tense, and peered into the window.

The fire burned about ten feet away, casting eerie light and shadow on green-robed figures gathered beyond. They were hooded, covered from head to knee—which was as far down as Sam could see. They stood in a circle, their arms raised and hands held.

They parted into two columns and as they did, Sam held her breath at the sight of a pale, naked woman on the ground between them. She was staked out, roped at wrists and ankles, completely exposed and helpless.

One of the robed figures stepped forward, holding a long dagger with a weird wavy blade. It caught the green fire and reflected it. The captive's eyes locked on the weapon.

The high priestess raised the dagger high, pointed it skyward, then plunged it into the girl's breast. It seemed to move in slow motion and Sam couldn't look away. The chanting continued as the priestess twisted the weapon. Blood spurted across her painted face, gushed up in a geyser. With an animal cry, the priestess rose, holding the captive's heart for all to see.

She licked blood from her lips.

And then her eyes locked on Sam's. . . .

Books by Tamara Thorne

HAUNTED

MOONFALL

ETERNITY

CANDLE BAY

BAD THINGS

THE FORGOTTEN

The Sorority Trilogy
EVE
MERILYNN
SAMANTHA

Published by Pinnacle Books

⊰THE SORORITY⊱
SAMANTHA

TAMARA THORNE

PINNACLE BOOKS
Kensington Publishing Corp.
http://www.kensingtonbooks.com

For Bill Gagliani,

*Boon Companion
and
Keeper of Rare Stories*

ACKNOWLEDGMENTS

Thanks go to:

My darling Damien, provider of the necessities of life, no matter how kinky they may be.

John Scognamiglio, for faith, patience, and making order out of chaos.

Kay McCauley, for taking care of business.

Heather Locke, for making my Web a site to behold.

Q.L. Pearce, for books and fun.

Chelsea Quinn Yarbro, for advice and fun.

Bill Gagliani, for always knowing weird things.

Brian and Leah, for understanding and doing the cooking.

Michele Santelices, Gerina Dunwich, Adam Contreas, Jim Beusse, Eric Hoheisele, and Brett Boyd for aid and inspiration in a rainbow of ranges.

The Orange Boys for applying decorative ginger fur to all my clothes.

Secret Societies for being so secretive.

The New World Order for providing so much basic horror material.

Monty Python and the National Lampoon for helping shape my adolescent view of Arthurian lore and Greek college societies.

And to the little handfuls of sorority girls and cheerleaders who alienated everyone, even their own squads and sisterhoods, with their shameless arrogance.

This one's on you, babes!

Applehead Lake Cheerleading Camp

Eight Years Ago

1

Meteors showered the black velvet night. *The Perseids.* Samantha Penrose lay on her back just inside the tree line not far from the cabins and tried to concentrate on the annual mid-August display.

It wasn't easy. Tree limbs blocked much of the view, but the only other place nearby—*the best place*—to view the meteor shower would be from the shadows of the dock or boathouse. *That's where you should be. What are you, a coward?*

Maybe I'm just smart. She wiggled a little, trying to get more comfortable on the loamy bed of ancient oak leaves and pine needles. After what she and Merilynn had seen under the water two nights ago, she really didn't want to approach the lake or its creaky old structures at night.

By herself.

You're chicken! taunted her inner bully.

No, I'm exercising caution! retorted her inner reporter.

Sam craned her neck as a bright flash fled across the sky and quickly disappeared behind the trees.

She knew all about people who weren't cautious; they were the ones who got killed when rock-climbing because they didn't bother to check their ropes, or murdered because they pretended it was safe to walk down a street alone even though everyone knew muggers struck there. If you had to do something risky, you went prepared, alert, confident, but as her father always told her, you darned well better not do it just to show off.

Lurking around the dock and boathouse would have been showing off. Definitely. And just standing out there in plain sight on the beach would be even stupider. *You know you don't want to go near that lake anyway.*

If she had brought anyone with her, she might have been tempted to approach the water, and that was part of the reason she'd slipped out of her cabin at one in the morning all alone. Her father always said that taking stupid chances had to do with your inner bully wanting to get loose and show off—or other people's inner bullies daring you to. He said it was more of a man thing, usually, but that she was a chip off his block, not Mom's, so she should learn from his mistakes.

He'd made lots of them, he told her. He couldn't resist a dare when he was young and ended up breaking his arm twice and his leg once. The worst was the time he'd gone up the stairs of the local abandoned "haunted" house (three stories of peeling white clapboard) while the other boys watched— that was when he broke his leg. It wasn't because of imagined ghosts or guys trying to scare him, but because his foot broke through one of the stairs and he crashed through the rotted wood halfway up his thigh before his leg snapped.

He was full of stories like that. He finally learned his lesson in Vietnam. Despite broken bones, sprains, stitches, and a concussion at the age of ten when he took—and won—a bet that he couldn't make his swing go over its A-frame in a complete circle, he had still believed, at nineteen, that nothing could kill him. He did all sorts of stupid things. Bullets barely missed him as he took chances the others in his squad wouldn't. He loved the feeling it gave him. But finally, shrapnel got him. Even now, Sam wasn't sure what shrapnel looked like, or even what it was, but she pictured hunks of twisted knives. The surgeons had removed pieces from his abdomen—he had shiny scars that were pretty cool looking—but they'd also had to remove his left hand and arm, halfway to his elbow.

That wasn't cool, not at all, and it was why she listened to him. His missing hand gave her nightmares when she was younger. Even now, sometimes. She shivered despite the warmth of the night. *Don't think about it!*

Thinking about things that scared you could get you into trouble, too. Old dreams about crawling hands climbing her bedspread, moving over her covers, dripping blood as the fingers moved steadily toward her neck, suddenly flashed through her head. The hand never looked like Thing in *The Addams Family*. The one in her dreams had a ragged, bloody stump, meaty, with white bone shards sticking out of it like needles.

Stop thinking about that! I have to be on alert. I can't let anyone catch me out here! Only two more

*days and this stupid camp is over. No more dumb
cheers. But if they catch me, they'll make me prac-
tice extra time until it's time to go home! Yuck!*

The horror that thought stirred was preferable to
the kind brought on by thoughts of severed hands. It
buoyed her, and she concentrated on the sliver of
sky visible between the trees. Soon, she felt no fear
at all, just irritation at how little of the sky show she
could see.

Quietly, she rose and brushed away the brown
leaves sticking to her legs and shorts. Walking to
the very edge of the forest, she stood in the shadows of the trees that met the lakefront beach—*don't
move, people who move get caught*—and studied
the sky. The still air, retaining dregs of daytime
warmth, smelled pleasantly of pine and earth. The
view here was much better, but it was easy to look
at the lake too, and she really didn't want to look at
it.

That's as silly as being afraid of a crawling hand.

She made herself look at the lake. It was a good
twenty yards distant. It gleamed darkly, a black
jewel, unfathomable. Far out, a low mist hung a foot
or two above the water. Undoubtedly, it shrouded
the island; she couldn't even see its silhouette. The
moon hung coyly low, flirting with the tops of the
trees, and what light it shed left Applehead Island
completely untouched.

Calm now, in control, Samantha returned her
gaze to the velvety clear night. Stars twinkled, plan-
ets glowed steadily. She picked out constellations;
Leo, the Big Dipper. Smaller, more distant, her favorite, the Pleiades. The Seven Sisters. Mythical, mag-

ical sisters. She liked mythology, especially Greek stories of gods and demigods.

The still warmth was broken abruptly by a stray breeze. It felt good against her face, holding a hint of coolness, no doubt from the lake, for it brought with it the faint dank cold-water smell. It gave her goose bumps, bringing the image of the ghost of Holly Gayle staring up at her from beneath the lake surface. *Stop it, right now! Maintain your control!*

The breeze continued, strengthened enough to ruffle her bangs, and she thought she heard faint voices come with it. *Singing?* It was too soft for her to be sure, but it made her think of times when the water pipes in her home vibrated just right. Her dad had explained how that worked, dispelling imagination with science, but it still reminded her of distant feminine voices singing, almost chanting. She thought that this was what the Sirens of myth sounded like as they lured sailors to their deaths.

Now, in the woods, the voices grew clearer but remained too faint to be truly recognizable as human. Not birds, no, but probably the wind vibrating leaves the way water sometimes vibrated through the plumbing. She cocked her head, forgetting the sky, enchanted by the music.

It sounded closer as the breezes increased.

Five minutes passed before she decided that what she heard really were voices. *Not too far away . . .* She was drawn to them. *I can walk along the edge of the forest. No one will see me.*

For an instant, she hesitated, wondering if she was being foolish, like the sailors who listened to the Sirens' call. *Maybe.* But as long as she stayed away from the lake and kept to the shadows and paid attention to where she stepped, why not? Reaching in her pocket to make sure the short-packaged lightstick hadn't fallen out—*I probably won't need to break it open, but I have to be prepared!*—she began walking toward the singing.

2

Skirting the lakefront, moving from tree to tree
away from the cheerleading camp, toward the voices
singing somewhere along the eastern side of the
lake, Sam imagined she was a native scout, sneaking
up on buffalo killers, then switched to pretending to
be Jane Bond, girl spy. By the time she had turned
to her favorite game—investigative reporter, about to
break open a story—the singing was very clear, though
she couldn't understand any words.

Forgetting the games, she paused to look back at
Applehead camp, seeing little but the sodium glow
of a few tall lamps among the trees, a suggestion of
a square building or two, the hulk of the boathouse,
and short length of dock. She wasn't sure how far
she'd come—*a quarter mile, an eighth?*—but the
camp looked small and far away. It lay at the short
south end of the oblong lake and she was well away
from there now, somewhere on the lower eastern side.

The song of the Sirens. Listening to the a cappella
voices, she felt a fresh surge of fear, but it passed
quickly. The choral music rose and fell, so beautiful,

so foreign. The tone grew more intense, stronger paced, as she listened. It was building to some sort of climax and the beauty and intrigue compelled her to move on despite the danger. *Alleged danger.*

No longer playing pretend, not even thinking of it, but relishing the adrenaline rushing through her, she kept to the shadows, as close to the edge as possible. It seemed darker here. *It is darker. You can't even see the moon from here!* She patted her light-stick, safe and sound in her pocket, but didn't even think of using it yet, not as long as she could see by the dim phosphorescent gleam of the pale beach sand.

The voices rose higher and stronger, flavored with a tinge of ugliness in the foreign words that stained the enchantment of the choir. She moved forward ten more feet and stopped. The music came from within in the forest—directly within.

There was a well-worn path to follow. She turned onto it and faced the trees, thinking that this was the end of the line. If she used the light-stick, someone might see it, but how could she walk into the trees in near blindness? *You can still see the path a little. Just stay on it and go a little ways. Just until you can't make it out anymore. It's what a smart reporter would do.*

Reporters, her father had told her when she asked, usually had much longer life spans than spies, and agreed that journalism would probably be a more rewarding career. When he said that, he was bandaging her magnificently skinned knee. Finished, he told her, *You have to be cautious now so that you can grow up and become what you want to be.*

The path was pale bare dirt, mixed with sand at first, and as long as she walked very slowly, she could make it out. The choral sounded closer, wilder yet still oddly religious. *Just a little ways farther,* she promised herself. *Stay in control, don't take risks.*

As she crept along, a slave to her curiosity, it suddenly occurred to her that these voices might not belong to students from the college or girls from camp, or even counselors. Sure, camps had sing-alongs, but this didn't sound like anything associated with roasting marshmallows.

Telling ghost stories, maybe.

She shivered and stumbled as the all but invisible path jogged. She paused, her eyes on the ground, her ears entranced, her nose full of earth and pine and lake smell. And fire. Just a hint. A campfire, a bonfire, but not a forest fire. Slowly, she became more aware of the trees pressing in on her, of the voices, singing so close—*it's the way the wind is blowing, they can't be that close!*—of the lack of other forest sounds. Nervously, she continued to look down, and could barely see tho outline of her shoes, let alone the path. *This is it. Time to turn back.*

And then she looked up.

In the woods, not too distant, she spotted a small square of firelight—*the bonfire.* It was as if she were looking at it through a window, but that didn't make sense, nor did the color of it—the flames, if that's what they were, had a greenish tint.

Sam realized she was trembling. *You can change the color of fire by tossing chemicals on it.* Or maybe it was just the green of the trees casting strange reflections. The chorus lowered, then rose again, frenzied, reminding her of church music, weird church music. And then she realized she was looking at the old chapel.

The haunted chapel.

A few days ago, she would have laughed off the haunted part. Now she wasn't so sure. Voices rose impossibly high and, for the first time, they reminded her of the banshee-howls on Applehead Island.

They don't sound anything like the howls did, her inner bully challenged.

No, but they still remind *me of them,* replied the wary investigator within.

She'd come so far that she decided to continue on. Soon the fiery greenish gleam coming from the window threw enough light to let her see the path. Silently, she moved forward and the size of the window grew quickly. She was nearly there. Singing filled the air. A few more steps and the trees ended, encircling a broad clearing the same way they did the lake. In the middle of the clearing stood the ruins of the chapel. *It's a make-out spot.* But it sure didn't sound like anyone was making out in there.

Swallowing, she crouched low and moved fast, covering the space to the window in twenty steps. She stayed slightly hunkered beneath it as she worked up her courage to look in. She took a deep breath, exhaled slowly, and studied what she could see of the building. There were actually two windows; this one, which had been her beacon, at one side of the small chapel, and another, just like it, at the other side. The blank center of the stone building must have once been behind the preacher's pulpit.

Slowly, slowly, she rose, leg muscles tight and tense, and peered into the window.

The fire burned about ten feet away, casting eerie light and shadow on green-robed figures gathered beyond. They were hooded, covered from head to knee—which was as far down as Sam could see. They stood in a circle, their arms raised and hands held. They continued to sing and Sam couldn't see what, if anything, was in the middle of the group. Rising higher, calf muscles trembling, threatening to knot, she saw their feet.

They were all floating a foot above the ground. *Nah, don't be ridiculous. Only half a foot.*

Sam nearly laughed, forced herself to maintain control. *No! Don't lose it. It's just a trick.*

She couldn't look away as the girls' song grew soft and they slowly floated to the ground.

They parted into two columns and as they did, Sam held her breath at the sight of a pale, naked woman on the ground between them. She was staked out, roped at wrists and ankles, completely exposed and helpless. A gag of green cloth invaded her mouth. Long blond hair spilled around her head. Her eyes rolled back in her head. *She sees me!*

One of the robed figures stepped forward, holding a long black dagger with a weird wavy blade. It caught the green fire and reflected it. The captive's eyes locked on the weapon.

The high priestess—*that's what she is, she must be some kind of high priestess, what else could she be?*—raised the dagger high, pointed it skyward, and as she did, her robe simply fell off. As if by magic. *Or a button came undone.*

But an instant later, all their robes fell to the ground. *Thirteen,* Sam counted. *There are thirteen of them.* They began their chant once more, and the high priestess, her face made up like an Egyptian queen's, moved forward, stepping between the legs of the captive, lowering herself to her knees.

The blade plunged into the girl's breast. It seemed to move in slow motion. Sam couldn't look away. The chanting crescendoed as the priestess twisted the weapon. Blood spurted across her painted face, gushed up in a geyser. With an animal cry, the priestess rose, holding the captive's heart up for all to see.

She licked blood from her lips. And then her eyes locked with Sam's.

Greenbriar University

University

TODAY

3

Samantha Penrose moved restlessly, deep in troubled sleep. In her dream, she heard screams and shrieks in the murky forest, but she saw nothing except dark shadowed tree trunks looming everywhere like monstrous prison bars. She tried to run from the horrible sounds, but her feet wouldn't obey, couldn't obey, and she moved in slow motion, fettered by tarry, grasping soil.

Determined, she kept trying to run, just as she had in dream after endless dream, all night long, but the forest floor sprouted fingers, hands that grabbed at her ankles and dug dirty nails into her flesh as the shrieking echoed through the trees. She pulled hard, tearing away from the hand, but it came with her, hanging on, trailing blood. More and more hands pushed up from the earth and tried to stop her, but she wouldn't stop and they pulled out of the ground like clumps of grass with foxtail fingers.

The hands grew among the ferns beneath the trees, everywhere, fields of them, grottoes of them, and the ones that weren't trying to catch her began to clap. The sound grew and grew until it was like thunder pounding all around her, thudding in time with her heartbeat, her pulse, faster and faster.

No! she yelled in the nightmare. *No!* A strong hand caught her, stopped her. She pulled but couldn't get away. Applause rumbled and rattled, filling her head.

"No!" Sam cried out loud, heart pounding as she jolted awake. Something held on to her ankle and she shook her leg hard, frantic to be free, nearly panicking before she realized the sheet had twisted around her leg.

Clapping. More adrenaline shot through her body.

"Sam?" Kendra Phillips called from beyond her door.

It's knocking, you idiot! Sam saw daylight seeping in from behind her thick curtains. Her alarm clock read 7:10 A.M. It would go off in five minutes.

"Sam?" Kendra's voice was hushed but urgent. She rapped on the door again.

"Just a minute." Sam turned off the alarm and untangled herself from the bedding. *What a mess.* Embarrassed—it was obvious that she'd been flailing around all night—she pulled her plum comforter over the mess, then ran her fingers through her hair and shook her body slightly to straighten the T-shirt and pajama pants she wore. "Come in."

Kendra opened the door, paused in the darkness. "I'm sorry. I woke you up, didn't I?"

"Better you than the alarm clock. The light switch is on your right." Sam crossed to her dresser and picked up her brush as she spoke.

"Sam, I have to show you something."

Sam whipped the brush through her dark hair and turned, alarmed by Kendra's tone. "What's wrong?"

Kendra touched the door, making sure it was latched, then crossed to Sam, holding out a piece of lined yellow paper. "Read this," she said softly.

For a brief instant, as she stared at Merilynn's graceful looping handwriting, Sam imagined she felt a cold disembodied hand grasping her ankle again. "'Kendra, I know where the knife with the stone is and I've gone to get it. Don't tell anyone. Love, Merilynn.'"

"I figured Merilynn wouldn't mind if I showed you," Kendra said as she took the note back, folded it, and put it in the pocket of her jeans. "She's gone."

4

"I don't understand. What's this business about a knife with a stone?"

Sam's room was a single, smaller than Kendra's, and with the dark curtains it felt claustrophobic. Kendra walked to the window and touched the plum-colored cloth. "May I?"

"Sure."

Behind her, Kendra heard Sam moving around, opening drawers, then the closet. Kendra let the morning sun in and stared down at the back garden, shivering slightly at the sight of the morning mist low above the lawn. She imagined spirits swirling within it as she heard Sam's pajamas land on the bed, and the distinctive swish of jeans sliding up legs. *It wasn't a dream,* she told herself, patting her pants pocket, very aware of the note folded inside it.

Sam made a little grunting sound and Kendra heard a bra hook snap closed, a shirt being pulled on, then footsteps as she came to join her at the window.

"So, what does the note mean?"

"I'm not sure, but Merilynn's gone and I've got a bad feeling about it." Kendra watched a crow swoop down and land on the lawn. It poked its beak at the ground. A moment later, two more shiny black birds joined it. The first one cocked its head and seemed to peer up at the window. *At me.* She turned toward Sam. "A *really* bad feeling."

"Why?" Sam was watching the birds now.

"Because something happened last night."

"Tell me."

"If I do, you can't repeat—" Kendra cut herself off, seeing the look on Samantha's face. There was no need to say it. "We were fooling around last night," she began.

Sam cocked her head, not unlike the crow. "Fooling around?" she asked slowly.

"Oh, Lord, no. I mean goofing off. I'm used to hearing my granny use those words. She doesn't mean . . . that."

"You might want to stop using the expression," Sam said, sounding amused, "unless you want to make some really close friends in this house."

Kendra smiled slightly. "You've noticed them too? Malory and Brittany?"

"Who couldn't notice?" Sam said. "I've tried to keep an eye on them. I'm almost positive they have a ménage à trois going with Professor Piccolo."

"Really?"

"Yeah, but what about Merilynn? What happened?" She paused. "You two didn't go back outside, did you?"

"No. You didn't happen to look out your window a little while after we left you, did you?"

"No. I always close the curtains. Why?"

"We saw them. Holly Gayle and Eve. Out there, on the lawn."

"You're kidding."

Kendra shook her head solemnly. "I swear it."

"Why didn't you come and get me?"

"We didn't think of it." She studied Sam. "Actually, Merilynn decided we should have a séance. I don't think she thought you'd want to join in."

Laughing, Sam shook her head. "I'll bet. So did anything happen? Did you call up something?"

"No. Nothing happened."

Sam's eyebrow went Spocky.

"Not then. Not until after we went to bed."

"And?"

"They came. We felt them first. The air turned cold and electrical—"

"Static electricity?"

Kendra nodded. "Then they just drifted into the room, plain as day. The lights were out, but I saw them. And there was the smell of water, sort of outdoorsy, know what I mean?"

"Lake water."

"You've smelled them?"

Sam's mouth crooked up slightly. "I don't know, but I do associate the smell of Applehead Lake with Holly Gayle. You know, from the story Merilynn told you about our little boat trip."

"I know. And that's what they smelled like. Eve looked just like she did when she disappeared. She had on that pink sweater and jeans. Holly was in the white dress. She looked wet."

"What happened then?"

"It was surreal. Eve spoke to me, in my head. Does that make sense to you?"

Sam nodded. "It does. What'd she say?"

"She warned me that I was in danger, that they'd killed her. Drugged her. They were going to sacrifice her to the Forest Knight."

"They? Who's they?"

"Holly said, 'The sorceress and her familiar.' Or something a lot like that. I think. It's a little blurry."

"Wait. Wait a second. Eve said they were *going* to sacrifice her? Not that they *had* sacrificed her?"

"Yes." Understanding dawned. "You're smart, you know that?"

Sam shrugged. "Maybe something went wrong. Maybe not. What else?"

Memories fled in and out of Kendra's mind. "I think Eve told me that Holly rescued her. Do you think she meant from Malory and Brittany?"

"I wouldn't be surprised. You know about the secret society, right?"

"Some, yes."

"I think they may do things like that."

"Sacrifice?"

"Yeah." Sam glanced at her wristwatch. "So, what else did they say?"

"It was weird. I faded out. I didn't want to. I mean I was awake one minute and sort of half asleep the next. Holly talked to Merilynn. I sort of heard it. She said something about the knight's daughter being able to rescue them. All of them." Kendra paused, shivered. "The ones under the lake. The ghosts."

"How?"

She shook her head. "I wish I could tell you. Suddenly, I couldn't keep my eyes open. It was like a dream, but I don't think it was. Holly showed Merilynn something. It was on the bodice of her dress. I didn't see it exactly, but she lifted the ruffles and there was something silver and a green glow."

"Green like the eyes?"

"I think so. But it was just one thing. Maybe a big brooch or something. A piece of jewelry, I'm almost sure. Or maybe a knife"

"A gemstone set in a miniature sword, maybe?" Sam asked.

"I think that's likely. I wish I could remember more. I think Holly said she'd tell Merilynn where to find it in a dream. It was really important. Damn it. I'm sorry. I should remember more."

"Well, keep thinking about it, but don't tell anyone else anything."

"I wouldn't any more than you would."

"I believe you. Don't write anything down either. There's no privacy here."

"I know."

"What are you going to do with the note?"

"I thought I'd contact her father. The priest?"
Sam nodded.

"I think he's involved in it. There was something said about him too." Kendra searched her memory, came up empty. "Damn it."

"Let's talk about it away from here. Later. I'm going to go get finished in the bathroom; then do you have time for some coffee and a donut or something?"

"Sure. Here?" They walked to the door.

"It's free here," Sam said. "We can go see what everyone's up to."

"What if they ask about Merilynn?"

The pair stepped into the hall. "We know nothing. She must have had an early class."

They paused outside the door, then turned toward the grand staircase, hearing voices coming from the east wing. Malory and Brittany.

"Hi, sisters," chirped the little blonde.

"Hi, Brittany," Sam said. "Hi, Malory."

Kendra echoed the words, and added, "How are you this morning?"

Brittany giggled and Malory glared. Neither replied, but as they reached the staircase and stepped down, a high-pitched *tweeeeeeeoot!* sound came from one of them, followed by a horrible stench.

Kendra backed up, Sam with her. As soon as the president and her VP were out of sight, Sam fanned the air. "No wonder Malory looked so sour."

"Something crawled up her ass and died." Kendra fought back a giggle.

"Yeah. About three days ago."

5

"God, what the hell happened here?" Jenny Goram asked Ginny Hill as they—the least senior pair of Fata Morganas—surveyed the carnage in the ruins of the Forest Knight's Chapel. The shiny skinless bodies twined together in a nest of blood-spattered grass, like food upchucked for gigantic baby birds by their mother. Or an Easter basket for a dragon.

"Brittany said the Forest Knight was angry at them, that *he* did this," Ginny said. "He wants his sacrifice."

Jenny nodded. She'd heard what Brittany had said, too. She just didn't want to believe it. Nor did she want to believe she and Ginny were in charge of getting rid of the remains. Shrugging out of her backpack, she forced herself to keep her eyes on the mangled bodies. "It's *so* gross."

"It is." Ginny opened her own pack and took out a folded camping shovel. "Eww," she added as she flipped it open and locked the joints. "Wow, this is cool. For a shovel, I mean. It's, like, a real shovel."

"Full-sized." Jenny opened her own, doing it carefully and slowly, an excuse not to look at the bodies they were supposed to bury. All too soon, she was ready to work. "So, do you have that map?"

Ginny took a folded piece of graph paper from her pocket and the girls turned from the tangle of bodies to study the diagram. It was a simple drawing of the chapel's interior, graphed off to show square footage. The door and window openings, the altar, and several other fairly permanent items—two piles of rocks, a log, the firepit—were marked. Other groups of squares were filled in as well; many others. Those, Brittany had explained when she awakened them shortly before dawn, were other graves. She had then marked six squares with blue pencil and told them to bury the new bodies strictly within the blue area.

Jenny got out the measuring tape Brittany had sent with them and before too long, the pair figured out where to dig and that they would only have to drag the corpses a little ways. "What a relief." Jenny hadn't even been sure they'd be able to figure out the measurements correctly, but Ginny turned out to be good at that sort of thing.

"We'd better get to work," Ginny said grimly as she stuck her shovel into the grassy earth.

Jenny did the same. "Do you think it's dangerous, burying them here? I mean, it's so obvious." She paused, turning to look in the direction of a series of squirrelish trills. "Ah, look! How cute!" She pointed at a little reddish brown chipmunk perched on a windowsill. Its brown and white stripes shone, highlighted by morning sunlight that peeped through the trees. In one delicate little paw, it held something bright yellow and slightly nibbled-looking.

"Oh, it's so sweet," Ginny cooed, then pitched her voice up to a squeak. "Hi, little guy!"

The rodent emitted a loud chirp and held its empty paw up at them, making the girls both giggle. "I think he's flipping us off," Ginny said. The rodent made another shrill noise and raised its little paw higher.

"I think *she* doesn't like being called a guy," Jenny said. "Right, sweetie?"

The chipmunk lowered its paw, trilled pleasantly, and set to work gnawing its yellow goodie. "See?" Jenny said, pushing her spade into the loamy earth. "She's a girl. I wonder what she's eating."

Ginny scooped dirt out of the ground, then peered at the chipmunk again. "I'm guessing it's a peanut M&M."

"Maybe she stole it from Brittany."

The chipmunk trilled merrily.

"I think she's laughing," Jenny said.

Ginny pushed her hair out of her face. "I wish I had a scrunchie. Let's get done before Brittany shows up to check on us."

Jenny nodded and worked. "I wonder why Brittany's in charge, not Malory or even Heather."

"Brittany's the only one who didn't look like shit this morning. Didn't you notice?"

"Yeah, you're right. But this seems like something Malory would want to oversee herself. Brittany's not exactly, you know . . ."

"What?" Ginny asked.

"Leadership material? I mean, she's more like, I don't know! Do *you* know what I mean?"

"She's cute," Ginny said. "Malory's more the leader type, but I think there's a lot more to Brittany than meets the eye. That dumb blonde act is just an act."

"Watch out!" Jenny laughed as the little chipmunk, the candy still in its mouth, raced from the window and up Ginny's leg.

Ginny stood still as the little thing hopped up to her shoulder, took the candy from its mouth, and chittered in her ear.

"She likes you," Jenny said.

The chipmunk held the remains of the candy out, pushing it toward Ginny's mouth.

"Ewww," Ginny said, disgusted.

"She's trying to share with you."

"It's a fucking rodent," Ginny said.

The chipmunk screeched, sank its teeth into Ginny's ear, then leaped onto Jenny's shoulder and held out the candy bit. Jenny opened her mouth and let the creature put the morsel on her tongue. It watched her carefully as she chewed and swallowed, then let out a happy series of trills and raced back to the window.

"I wonder if I need a rabies shot," Ginny moaned, holding her ear.

"Let me see. Let go."

"Okay. How bad is it?"

"She didn't even break the skin," Jenny said. "It's barely red, even." She paused. "Those little ground squirrels have incredibly strong jaws. I think she was just teaching you a lesson. She could have taken your earlobe off if she'd wanted to."

Ginny looked over at the chipmunk sunning itself on the window sill. "Maybe. Or maybe it's just a stu—"

"Shh!" Jenny hushed.

"What?"

"Just be quiet and work. Count your blessings."

"But that—"

"That chipmunk is so adorable it's hard to work," Jenny finished quickly, suddenly nervously aware of the little creature's shiny black button eyes. She didn't understand why, but she had the feeling it understood their every word. One of the reasons she'd been accepted into the inner circle of Gamma, the Fata Morgana, was her ability to intuit things, and she knew enough to listen to herself now.

6

Kendra waited for Sam on the upstairs landing, enjoying the morning sunlight that strobed across the gleaming wood risers and the floor below. The old house looked fresh this morning, and the sounds of sorority sisters bustling around downstairs seemed lively and normal. She thought she could smell the rich fragrance of coffee wafting up the stairs, but there was a foul odor beneath it, one that overwhelmed the usual lemony wax smell of the polished wood and the funereal odor of roses.

"Hey," Sam said, joining her. "The bathrooms are zoos. Sorry I was so slow. Petra Mills shares my bathroom. Do you know her?"

"No."

"She's a senior. She's always slow, but today, Lord! And whatever Malory ate, she must have had some too. I had to hold my breath to brush my teeth, and I'll tell you, that's not easy to do."

"Is Petra a cheerleader?"

"No, why?" Sam asked.

Kendra shrugged.

"Gods!" shrieked Heather Horner as she appeared from the recesses of the east wing, the look on her pasty face as nasty as the sound of her voice. "Shit!" she snapped, then saw Sam and Kendra watching her. "Do either of you have a tampon you can lend me?"

"I'll give you one, but I don't want it back." Sam opened her book bag and started digging around the bottom, soon came up with a slender white-wrapped item and handed it Heather, who didn't look amused.

"Thanks."

"Got a surprise visit from Aunt Flo?" Kendra asked in her most sympathetic tone.

Heather rolled her eyes, emphasizing the dark shadows beneath them, then started to shake her head, but stopped abruptly.

Hangover, Kendra thought with a mean little twist of satisfaction.

"I'm way early. I'm always like clockwork. I don't know what happened. Damn it. I had plugs, you know?" she added, using the wrapped one as a pointer as she spoke. "Half a fucking box of the things, but every last one of them fell apart on me."

Kendra tried to appear concerned. "I'm sorry, Heather."

"You should complain to the manufacturer," Sam added in her reporter voice.

More eye rolling commenced. "Yeah, a lot of good that's going to do me right now." She put one hand over her stomach. "I feel awful."

"Cramps?" Kendra asked.

"Not that kind," Heather replied in a pained voice. "I think it's something I ate." A delicate machine gun *tat-tat-tat-tat-tat* burst from her behind.

"Shit, I'm sorry. I've been like this since I woke up. Maybe I just drank too much last night."

Before Kendra could stop her, Sam said, "You and Malory must have had the same drink then."

Kendra stepped back as Heather's nether fragrance bloomed again.

"She's got gas, you mean?"

"Unless someone knows how to throw farts, she does."

Heather gave Sam a dirty look and stuck the tampon in her pocket. "Thanks," she said over her shoulder as she turned on her heel and headed back into the off-limits wing.

"What's so funny, Kendra? I thought you were going to have a fit right in front of her."

Kendra loosed a broad grin. "Merilynn did it," she whispered.

"Did what?"

"Wished twenty-four hours of flatulence on all the senior Gammas."

"What?"

"You know, she threw a spell on them the same way she popped the wrestlers' tires and called the deer. She did it."

"Possibly," Sam replied slowly. "Or it could be a coincidence."

"We'll know when we go downstairs, won't we? And, Sam?"

"Yes?"

"I don't think it's a coincidence. She did a period spell too."

"To all the seniors?"

"No. Just the cheerleaders. She gave them all their

periods and cursed their hygiene products." She grinned. "Double curses."

Sam snorted. "You're kidding."

"No," she said, smiling. "I thought it was a joke. Evidently, it isn't."

"Well, let's go down and have some breakfast," Sam said, stepping toward the staircase. "We'll do a little investigating on the sly."

"You really have a nose for news," Kendra said, hefting her book bag.

Sam let out a half a chuckle. "I'd say you're not bad at smelling a story yourself."

7

"What are we going to do about Michele?" Heather asked, swilling her second glass of purple juice, alcohol-free, this morning. "We have to do something. There's a game tonight."

Malory barely looked up from her coffee. "You're in charge of the fucking cheerleaders," she muttered as she tilted slightly to let a silent-but-deadly take flight. How could her body betray her like this? She'd tried spells and Gas-X and Pepto Bismol, but nothing would quiet her gut.

"You should have some juice," Heather said. "It'll perk you right up."

Malory shot her a killing look. "That stuff tastes like piss to me."

"Piss? You drink lemon juice without sugar, you're a fine one to talk— Lord, what died in your ass?"

"Don't start on the juice thing, Heather." She paused. "And you don't smell so great yourself. Maybe it was the vodka."

"Maybe. Anyway, I got my period," Heather replied. Malory ignored her.

"Why do I still have to get a period after all these years?"

"You stopped aging. If you'd stopped aging at sixty, you wouldn't have a period. Haven't we been over this before?"

"Do you still get a period?"

"Don't be an ass. Do I look like I don't?"

Heather let out a percolator-fart. "Sorry. Did you get yours this morning?"

"My what?"

"Your period."

"No."

"Huh."

"What's that supposed to mean?"

"I don't know. Brittany said that when she got Ginny and Jenny up to go do the dirty work, they were both on the rag and complaining about it."

"Good morning, Petra," Malory said, relieved to see the senior Gamma enter the kitchen.

"Good morning," Petra said, heading for the coffee-maker. "Lord, what stinks?"

"Sorry," Heather said, covering for Malory. Heather always did know exactly how to make points with the boss.

"Do you guys have any Midol?" Petra asked, sitting down.

"No."

"No."

"Shit. Nobody does."

"Nobody does what?" Sam Penrose asked as she and Kendra Phillips entered the huge kitchen.

"Has Midol," Heather replied. "Do you?"

"No."

"Sorry," added Kendra.

Malory let out another silent-but-deadly as the freshmen girls got themselves coffee and day-old donuts. She watched as the pair approached the table, smiled as Kendra's nose wrinkled.

Samantha's didn't twitch. "Where is everyone this morning?"

"It's early," Malory replied, sitting up straighter, curious about Samantha's thoughts.

"True," Sam said. "Usually Jenny and Ginny are down here before I am. And Julie and Jeannie and Michele." She smiled at Heather. "I've noticed that you cheerleaders are early risers."

Heather looked at Malory for guidance, but didn't get any. "I guess we usually are."

"Even Brittany's missing," Sam said lightly.

"She's off on her morning jog," Malory said, watching Sam. "She always goes out in the morning." She eyed the girl. "Surely, you've noticed that, being so into investigative reporting and all."

Sam looked her in the eye. "Yes, I have. But don't call me 'Shirley.'"

Kendra and Petra both snickered, but Sam never cracked a smile.

Malory gave her a little nod of approval.

"Oh, sorry!" Heather said as she ripped off another percolator imitation.

"How do you feel?" Malory asked, looking from Petra to the freshmen. "Before you arrived, Heather and I were comparing notes on what we ate last night. We think we may have a little food poisoning. Upset stomachs. Did any of you eat here last night?"

"I had a Lean Cuisine," Petra said. "Nothing else. I'm fine."

"We went out for pizza," Kendra said.

Malory nodded. She'd been told by other Fatas that they'd been out; Merilynn and Sam were two girls she liked to keep a special eye on. "Did Merilynn go with you?"

"Yes," Kendra replied after the briefest hesitation.

Sam never blinked, but Malory felt suddenly suspicious. "Where is she this morning? I take it she's all right?"

There was no mistaking the brief flare of nostrils and constriction of pupils on Kendra, and even Sam wasn't able to completely hide a reaction. She was so good, though, that Malory thought Heather was probably fooled. But she could tell something was up.

"Merilynn's fine," Kendra said. "She took off so early that I hardly remember hearing her leave."

I'll bet you don't. "Early class?"

"I guess," Kendra replied, a shade too quickly this time.

Sam briefly laid her hand on Kendra's forearm. "No, it wasn't a class, not exactly, remember, Kendra?"

Kendra opened her mouth but Sam spoke again, touched her again. "Of course you don't remember. You were in the rest room. She had an early class, but not *that* early," she said, turning her steady gaze on Malory. "She wanted to go sky-watching. There was some sort of planetary alignment she was interested in."

Kendra's smile and nod seemed genuine. "She loves astronomy. Or maybe astrology. Her bedspread is blue with stars and moons," she added, her own eyes surprisingly steady as they met Malory's. I don't know her all that well yet."

Very nicely done. So nice, Malory thought, that

she might even be telling the truth. "Merilynn just moved in with you, didn't she?"

"Yes, she did."

"I was surprised. I didn't know you even knew one another."

Kendra didn't reply, but half smiled and half shrugged, then took a bite of donut.

"How did you meet?" Heather asked, ignoring Kendra's full mouth.

"They're Gamma sisters, initiated together," Sam said serenely. "How could they *not* meet?"

Heather looked annoyed, but maybe that was just the gas.

Malory smiled warmly. "Well, I'm glad Merilynn is all right. We wouldn't want you to get a reputation, Kendra."

"A reputation?"

"You know what I mean, sweetie," she replied, all silk and sugar.

"No, I don't. A reputation?"

"As a jinx," Heather said.

Malory chuckled softly. "That's too strong a term. I just mean that when a girl goes through a lot of roommates, sometimes people get nervous about rooming with her."

Kendra studied Malory carefully, revealing little but a flash of well-tethered anger in her eyes. "You're speaking as though Merilynn has disappeared. I don't appreciate that, and neither would Merilynn."

Bravo! Kendra Phillips had never been retiring, but the courage she displayed now was new. *Most likely, Samantha's influence.* "I'm sorry," Malory told her. "That came out wrong. I didn't mean to imply anything. It's just that I don't feel quite myself this morning. Neither does Heather."

Heather nodded peevishly.

"Any of you guys have some Pepto Bismol or Maalox?" Teri Knolls moaned as she entered the kitchen. She was dressed in a Gamma megaphone sweater and jeans, and was holding her abdomen. "I don't feel so good." She went for the coffee, muttering, "And Midol. I need Midol."

8

"You bitch!" Nancy Mayhew squawked at her roommate, Diane Jespam. Actually, she squawked at Diane the Spam's big fat ass, which was all she could see of her since the Anna Nicole–wanna-be had her torso hidden in the recesses of Nancy's closet. She was rooting through her clothes like a pig roots for truffles. Nancy heard an audible snort as Diane pulled out of the depths and looked at her with smeared lipstick.

No doubt smeared all over my clothes.

The Spam blinked her false eyelashes, all breathy like Marilyn Monroe force-fed Crisco for a month. "What did you call me, Nancy? A witch?"

"A bitch," Nancy said evenly. "With a b. I called you a *bitch*."

"That's not very nice."

"I don't *feel* very nice." Nancy had awakened to find her period had come early and her sheets were stained. She was out of tampons and the stick-um on the emergency pads she dug out of the recesses of her bureau didn't stick. She'd ended up using mask-

ing tape on the damned things. *That's real attractive.*
As usual, she had cramps, and there was a football
game tonight. And now her asshole of a roommate
was scrounging through her closet—like she'd even
fit into anything Nancy owned.

She took a deep breath and counted to three, trying to push the fury she felt back down into stomach. Rarely had she felt such anger. *Super PMS?*
"What are you doing in *my* closet, Diane?"

"You're wearing your cheerleading clothes
tonight, right?"

"So?"

"So, I have a date tonight and I wanted to borrow
your sweater set."

"Oh?"

"The baby blue?" The Spam fluttered her polyester
lashes. "It's really more appropriate for my skin tone
than yours, you know."

"And the fact that you weigh fifty pounds more
than I do?"

"Hey! That's mean!"

"Did you factor that in?" Nancy persisted. "All
that flab? Do you really think you could squeeze
your pork into *my* sweater set without ripping it?"

Diane's too-red lower lip pooched out. "You're
mean! Sweaters stretch, you know." She turned back
to the open closet. "For those of us with feminine
bustlines, anyway."

"They. Only. Stretch. So. Far." Nancy took another deep breath. "Get out of my closet, you walking cellulite factory."

Diane Jespam didn't even turn to look at her. "I'll
be done in a minute."

Nancy saw red filtering into her vision, coloring

everything she saw, especially Diane the Spam's lardy ass. Her cottage cheese cheeks billowed white, then pink, then seemed to turn as red as roses around a black thong that struggled against strangulation in her ass-crack. "You're done *now*," Nancy announced.

Diane turned, did her pout. "Come on, Nanny. Don't be so *mean*. We're *sisters!* And roommates. What's mine is yours and what's yours is mine. You know that, Nanny."

"I warned you not to call me that." Nancy stepped forward and yanked Diane's wrist, pulling her away from the closet.

"Hey—"

"I *don't* want anything of yours and you *can't* have anything of mine. Now take your filthy hands off my stuff or I'm going to knock that little piggy nose right off your face."

"Hey, my daddy paid seven thousand dollars for this nose! It's *perfect!*"

Nancy's world was suddenly awash in red, drenched in crimson tones of blood. Diane Jespam's blood. It felt hot and it felt good as she flattened her free hand and rammed it as hard as she could, up against the Spam's nose.

The girl's eyes widened, her face exploding in blood. The crunching sounds were very, *very* loud.

Diane Jespam dropped like a two-hundred-pound sack of potatoes. Blood ran into her open eyes. Her dead, staring eyes.

Her vision no longer infused with scarlet, Nancy bent and wiped her hand clean on the Spam's ass cheek, then went into the adjoining bathroom and washed properly before returning to the bedroom. Stepping over the body, marveling at how it was true—that you really could kill someone by squashing their nose up into their brain—she rifled through Jespam's drawers until she came up with a brand-new box of tampons.

Feeling triumphant, she decided that as soon as she finished dressing, she should talk to Heather. As the newest member of the squad—edging Little Lou out for Eve Camlan's vacated position—she knew that the head of the squad would be her best friend and advisor now.

9

"I think Malory knows something," Kendra told Sam Penrose when they met for lunch in a quiet corner of the cafeteria. It was still half an hour before noon, but the place was filling up fast.

Sam had picked the table for the view it gave of the entire eatery, and she'd picked her chair because it put her back to the wall. It was something her father had taught her when she was a kid. *Always be on the lookout, Sam. Keep your back to the wall and no one can sneak up on you.* She lifted her ham on wheat. "She knows something about Merilynn, you mean?"

Kendra nodded as she chewed the first bite of her hamburger, then set it on the plate and opened it. "Yes, about Merilynn." She removed half the onion and a thick spine of lettuce, then put it all back together again. "What do you think?"

"I *think* she was fishing," Sam told her. "I also think she was trying to get reactions out of us."

"Did she? Get a reaction out of me, I mean? You were a complete rock." She tried the burger again.

"Thanks, but I wasn't a complete rock. I'm not that good, but I tried. And, yes, I think she was able to get some reaction out of you, but not enough to really put her on to anything." She waved a Frito at Kendra. "You're really pretty smooth."

"Thank you. I wish I were as smooth as you."

Sam felt her eyebrow go up. It was an old movement she'd picked up as a kid watching Sean Connery in James Bond movies. When she was seven or eight, she spent hours pretending to be the master spy, and that eyebrow thing was part of the play. Now, she couldn't help it. Her father had explained to her when she was fourteen and worried about scaring off a junior nerd she liked, that the lift was a learned motion and very hard to get rid of. He said she could, but it would take concentration. Then he told her he liked it because it made her look smart.

Well, then she really tried to get rid of it for a while—no fourteen-year-old girl, not even she, wanted to look too smart. It would scare off boys. Fortunately, she'd soon met one that was as smart as she was and was also compelled to try to prove that he was not her equal but her better. She played along at first, keeping her eyebrow at bay, but being dumb wasn't her style and before long her competitive streak won out and she trumped the guy. Put him in his place. Raised her eyebrow. Robby, that was his name, liked the eyebrow and told her she was as hot as a female Vulcan. He called her Ms. Spock. *God, I loved that. Thank heaven I can take that fact to my grave!*

At the time, the Trekiness didn't seem geeky; it felt cool. And being smart and logical was great; Robby respected her for it. He backed off for a time, but after a while, he just had to prove how smart he was again. She egged him on, and then she trumped him again, twice. He fought back, trumped her. Three times. For a few brief, wonderful weeks, it was all-out war with mad necking sessions stolen in remote corners of the campus, under bleachers, behind trees, between the battles. They were both part-nerd, not quite outcasts, but never popular either, and between them they brought zero romantic or sexual experience to their hot little war.

Sam couldn't tell her father what was happening—she was too embarrassed. She couldn't tell her mother, because she would have gone all fluttery and weird on her. But the thing was, Sam knew herself, she always had known herself, and so she knew she would go all the way with him soon—just thinking about the intellectual battles left her with soggy underwear. She knew she would be the aggressor, too, and it was just too humiliating. She didn't want to go all the way—there were too many risks she wasn't prepared for, but that wasn't the big thing. She could figure that out if she had to. No, the *really* big thing she couldn't quite comprehend, the thing she couldn't bring herself to ask her father about, was why using her brain like that—to spar, to compete—was the one thing that she knew would make her lose control of herself physically.

It was just too illogical. Why would using her brain make her want to have sex? She should be able, she thought, to use her brain to make herself *not* want to have sex.

So, she stopped it herself by relentlessly ramming Robby into the ground. She hated doing it because she cheated, making things up, twisting facts, whatever she had to do, to win. Finally, she succeeded in driving him away.

"Sam? Earth to Sam?"

"Sorry. What?"

"You raised your eyebrow. I asked why."

"Oh, just an old *Star Trek* habit," she fibbed. "I can't break it," she added truthfully. "I try to raise the other one, but it won't cooperate."

Kendra laughed. "You're blushing. I didn't know anything could make *you* blush."

Flustered, Sam gulped Pepsi.

"I wasn't asking about your eyebrow, Sam. I was asking why you raised it when I said you were smooth."

It was the James Bond thing. James Bond was smooth. Why didn't I just tell her that? Why did I blame it on the Vulcans? "I don't know why; maybe because I don't feel all that smooth. Or maybe I wondered why you paid me a compliment."

Kendra didn't hide her irritation. "I'm no buttkisser. If I say something, I mean it."

"I know. I wouldn't be sitting here with you if I thought that. My words just didn't come out quite right." She smiled slightly. "That's one of the reasons I'd rather write than talk. It's easier to edit myself that way."

Kendra nodded. "I bet Merilynn drove you nuts the way she'd just say whatever she was thinking."

Sam grinned broadly. "I've enjoyed her lately, but that summer at the cheer camp, I totally wanted to strangle her every five minutes or so. But she was also sort of refreshing. She could make me laugh, and she was tough, even if she was a nutcase half the time. She never worried . . . " She studied Kendra and wondered if her stomach had started flopping like her own. "I'm talking about her like she's gone."

"She is." Kendra paused. "But I know what you mean. Like she's gone for good."

"She's just taken off on one of her adventures."

"Yeah."

Kendra looked pale despite her mocha complexion, and this brought Sam's mind back to the point she wanted to make. "I thought Malory probably read a little from your reactions this morning."

"Yes?"

"There was one thing in particular that you reacted to, and if Malory's as bad as I think she is, she'll keep using it. She senses weakness and goes for it every time. I've seen her do it lots of times, usually in small ways."

"For Christ's sake, spit it out! What's my weakness?"

"She played dirty."

"Just tell me. I can take it."

Sam felt her eyebrow lift of its own accord. "I believe you can."

"So?"

"Malory suggested that you could be considered a jinx as a roommate."

"Suggested it? Girl, she said it outright."

"And you reacted."

"No. I mean, inside, but I kept it inside. That was a nasty thing to say."

"You *almost* hid it. You hid your reaction better than ninety-five percent of people could, I think. But she startled you. You have to learn to control every tiny eye movement, even the flare of your nostrils. I can't do that." She paused. "Of course, I can't control my eyebrow either."

"I bet you can if you have to. *Really* have to."

Sam nodded. "But nostrils flare to get more oxygen when you're upset. Eyes widen—or squint, depending. There all these little tiny responses that neither you nor I can truly control. Only a really great actor or a sociopath can control things like that. You have to completely turn off emotionally to be completely armored."

"But if you do that, you don't pick up on everything around you."

"Exactly," Sam said.

"So, what do you think my reaction told Malory?"

"Not enough. I think she was trying to find out if we knew anything worth keeping secret. That jab at you was meant to elicit a big reaction—she was getting desperate. You did react, but it wasn't big—it was a normal reaction to an obnoxious, rude comment." Sam finished off her soda. "I'm getting a refill. You want one?"

Kendra nodded. "Iced tea. No sugar."

Sam took the cups and rose. "When I get back, I want you to tell me every detail about what you two did last night."

"Deal."

10

"This is quite a mess you've made," Malory Thomas told Nancy Mayhew as she, Heather, and Brittany stood in the freshman cheerleader's room and looked at the pudgy blond mess that had been the fairly unbeloved legacy sister, Diane Jespam, before Nancy, also a legacy but much more desirable, had flattened her face.

Nancy, clad in navy pants and a baby-blue sweater set, stared at her toes and nodded wordlessly.

Heather had been collared by Nancy shortly after breakfast and Malory, having gone back to bed with a hot water bottle, forgot all about them both until Heather knocked on the door to her room and told her what their impetuous little sister had done.

It had really improved Malory's mood. After discussing everything again with Brittany, they had gone back to the room, where Nancy obediently sat waiting at her desk, not a dozen feet from her victim's body.

Now Malory said, "Nancy?"

"Yes?" she mumbled.

"Look at me."

Slowly the girl raised her head. Her eyes were red-rimmed and puffy from crying. "Wipe your nose." Malory handed her a tissue and waited while the girl did as ordered.

"Nancy, why did you kill your roommate?" she asked in her best Elementary School Teacher voice.

"I'm sorry."

"I didn't ask you if you're sorry, Nancy. I asked why you did it. No, no. Look at me." She gently but firmly put her finger under Nancy's chin and forced her head back up.

"I was mad. I'm sorry. I got my period and I get really cranky when I get it and I just lost my temper."

"What did she do that made you angry?"

Nancy's lower lip trembled and a tear escaped one eye. Malory wiped it away with her finger. Nancy kept her chin up. "She was going through my closet." More tears leaked.

Malory gave her a fresh tissue. "I'll bet she was doing it without your permission. Am I right?"

"Yes!" Finally, Nancy's spirit flashed in her eyes, betraying the anger. "That cow wanted to borrow my—this." She touched the finely knit tank and matching sweater. "It's silk! And she didn't ask, she never asks, she just takes things, and she ruins them because she's a big fucking fat cow."

Nancy's shoulder shook seismically and she began sobbing out loud. Malory gathered her into her arms and let her get mucus and tears all over her own shoulder. It was disgusting, but part of the job. She murmured and stroked Nancy's hair soothingly until she calmed down. Fortunately, she had already had several hours to cry and it didn't take long before she dried up.

"Malory?" she asked. "What's going to happen to me now? Are you going to call the police?"

"You really shouldn't have killed her, Nancy," she said reprovingly.

"I know. I didn't mean to."

"We probably should turn you in. I think you're just a tiny bit insane."

"I'd rather be in a crazy house than in jail," the murderess said hopefully.

Malory slipped her arm around Nancy's shoulders and turned her away from the body. Together, they looked out the window that opened over the front of the house, giving a long view of the reflecting pond. "Nancy, you're a sister of Gamma Eta Pi. You're one of our own. You took vows."

Nancy nodded and wiped her nose.

"The sisters of Gamma Eta Pi protect one another within the limits of the law. Sometimes beyond. But murder, that's a little further beyond than we're willing to go. . . ."

Nancy took a deep breath, expelled it with a shudder. "I understand."

"No, sweetie, I don't think you do. Within Gamma, there is a secret core, the very heart of the sorority. We of the society of Fata Morgana protect one another from everything but doing harm to one another." She paused, letting her words sink in but resisting the impulse to weave a spell around the girl. To be a Fata Morgana, she had to go in with her eyes open.

"A Fata Morgana is a special Gamma, one who is

able to do things far beyond the realm of a normal sister. She is required to make sacrifices. And I don't mean silly things like burning your bra—"

"Huh?"

"Sorry, wrong decade. I don't mean silly things like getting your breast implants removed. I mean *real* sacrifices. Blood sacrifices. Like what you did here. Can you do that again?"

"What?" Nancy's eyes had turned to saucers. Bloodshot saucers, but Visine would clear that up before tonight's football game.

"Was Diane the first person you ever killed? Don't answer yet. If you have any desire to join our society, you must tell the absolute truth and, trust me, I'll know it if you're lying. Now, was she your first?"

"You mean human? Chickens don't count?"

"Chickens?"

"I tried voodoo, but my grandmother caught me in her henhouse and that was that."

Malory smiled. "What about humans?"

"Well, I'm not sure."

"Why don't you tell me about it?"

"Not a really long time after she caught me killing a chicken, my grandmother asked me to bring her her pills and a glass of water. She was sitting in the dark—she had a migraine and was really miserable—and I brought her some pills. She took them without looking. She died."

"What did you bring her?"

"I don't know," Nancy admitted. "Just sort of a pupu platter. One of these, two of those."

"So you weren't trying to kill her?"

She shrugged. "I don't know. I mean, she took all

these vitamins and supplements too, so it was a lot of pills. All she had to do was turn on the light and she would have known I didn't bring any vitamins, just heart medications and migraine pills and tranquilizers. Lots of those. They felt just like her vitamin C capsules."

"So you did it on purpose?"

"No, well, yes. I was just testing her. She didn't pass the test."

"And what happened next?"

"She got all strange and funky and told me to call 911."

"And did you?"

"Well, yes. But first I sat down at the kitchen table and played solitaire until I won three games in a row. Then I called."

"How many games did you play before you won three times running?"

Nancy looked at her, a trembling smile on her lips. "Only twenty-three."

"Nancy, dear, you aren't a nut. You're an entire basketful of nuts."

"Is that good?"

"It's just fine, as long as you want to become a Fata Morgana."

"Can I ask one question?"

"Of course."

"What does 'Fata' mean? It sounds fat. I hate fat."

"It has nothing to do with fat. Fata Morgana is Italian for Morgan LeFay. It also is a type of mirage."

"A mirage?"

"You know, something that appears to be something else?"

Nancy nodded. "I like that a lot. Who's Morgan LeFay? Is he the president of your society?"

"*She* is your new goddess, and yes, you could say she is president. She is a great sorceress, immortal, just as you shall be if you are loyal to her."

"I have to worship a goddess?"

"Yes, but you'll enjoy it. You'll have a god as well. It is he that we make sacrifices to in order to maintain our youth and beauty."

"Who is he?"

Malory gestured toward the woods, dark and forbidding even at midday. "The Forest Knight is your new god. Now, come, we will prepare you."

They turned. Under her arm, Nancy flinched slightly at the sight of Diane. "What about her?"

"Don't you worry a bit about her. We have ways to dispose of bodies. Many ways. This one, though, looks especially nice and tender, so I think, Brittany, if you'll give the good sisters down in Moonfall a call and see if they're in the market, we'll let them turn her into their famous mincemeat pies."

"Sisters in Moonfall? Is there a Fata Morgana society there?"

"No, they're another sort of sisterhood, but they're lots of fun."

"Will I meet them?"

"Not unless we need to turn you into mincemeat. And that won't happen, will it, Nancy?"

"Never!"

11

Sam finished her afternoon classes with her mind barely in attendance. All she could think about was Merilynn Morris. There were Kendra's stories about their seeing the ghosts to ponder, and Merilynn's spell-casting at the Gammas' expense to mull over, but what consumed most of her ability to concentrate were her own memories of the previous night. Because of them, she could not deny Merilynn's powers—she had seen them used twice last night and try as she might, she couldn't write off everything as coincidence. She wished that she could. Despite the fact that she trusted Kendra was telling her the truth as she interpreted it, she still would have been able to dismiss those tales if she hadn't seen Merilynn in action herself.

Yet it was the unearthly shrieks and screams that had come from deep within the dark forest the previous night that her mind wandered back to over and over again.

The sounds and Merilynn's reaction to them. The reaction was all wrong. Abnormally wrong. Sam's own instinct had been to run, as far and as fast as possible, and she trusted her instincts; they had never been wrong.

That Merilynn practically tried to pull them deeper into the woods was aberrant behavior. Sure, she lacked caution and possessed enough curiosity to damn a hundred cats, but that didn't explain her stunning lack of fear.

Kendra had felt it; they spoke of it at lunch. Merilynn insisted it was the cry of the Greenbriar Ghost, the Forest Knight himself. Certainly, it was the sort of feeling that legends were made of, a terror felt cold and deep inside your bones, something that could not be understood if it hadn't already been experienced. It was like a new color of fear, a new scent of terror. *A green face,* Sam thought. *The face of the forest, fear in shades of green and gold, scented with earth and pine and black lake water.*

Stop that. You're thinking like Merilynn!

Sam turned her mind, trying to consider the terror she had experienced logically, unemotionally. She knew she had felt it several other times, long ago. The first time had been while fleeing the island in the rain, after she saw those green-glowing eyes, when she heard that never-to-be-forgotten banshee wailing.

The second was in the boat with Merilynn, not when she saw the beautiful ghostly town, nor even when she first encountered Holly Gayle's white face staring up at her from just beneath the lake's surface, but when Merilynn had yanked her away from the phantom hand that was about to pull her below. The instant she had come out of the fugue state or trance or whatever the hell had hypnotized her into unthinking fearlessness, she felt the terror and knew how close to death she had come.

Is that how Merilynn felt last night? Was she in a trance, unable to even feel fear?

She reached the sidewalk that led to Gamma House and turned, barely glancing at the oblong reflecting pool, only vaguely aware of the beauty of the sparkling sunlight bouncing off the dark water and dancing over the lily pads. *Was Merilynn entranced? Hypnotized?* But certainly the shrieks hadn't caused her own trance; there had been no cries that night. Her instincts told her that she had been held spellbound by the eyes of Holly Gayle.

Now, as she approached the steps, Sam cruised rapidly through her memories, knowing she had felt the terror at least one other time. *Worse, worse terror than the other times.* The memory resisted her search momentarily, but then she captured it. *It was the night I went out to watch the Perseids meteor showers.* The stark remembrance stirred goose bumps up on her neck and arms as she mounted the stairs and stepped onto the veranda. *I heard it that night. The shrieks of the Greenbriar Ghost.*

There was more. She had wandered, gotten lost. *There was singing. The Sirens' song!*

Samantha!

Sam whirled at the voice, just behind her, but saw no one.

Samantha!

She opened her mouth to call, *Merrilynn!* but caught herself. *I'm going to give her holy hell for scaring me like this.* Sam looked over the edge of the veranda, but the redhead wasn't there. She let her gaze travel over the lawn, across the reflecting pond, and to the forest's edge. Nothing.

Samantha!

Sam thought she caught a flash of movement among the trees. Shading her eyes, she squinted at the shadowy borderland. Yes, something flickered red, a stray sunbeam. And there, suddenly, pale against the forest, she saw a faint, lithe figure, saw brilliant coppery hair blowing in a phantom breeze. She could almost see the green of her eyes. The figure, dressed in some sort of flowing lavender cloak or gown—it was too far away to be sure—raised one arm and waved.

"Merilynn," she murmured, and waved back. The figure faded away like smoke borne away on a breeze.

12

"Okay," Heather Horner said, startling Sam. "I got here in time to see you wave, but I don't see anyone."

The cheerleader, dressed in her two-piece baremidriff uniform, must have come out of the house, but Sam hadn't heard her. *You were too busy seeing ghosts to hear her.* The thought sank in an instant after it passed through her mind. *Merilynn? A ghost?*

"What's wrong, Sam?" Heather asked, joining her at the railing. "I've never seen you at a loss for words before."

"Oh, sorry. I was lost in thought. What did you say?"

"I asked who you were waving at," Heather said, the friendly tone disappearing. "You couldn't have been too lost in thought if you could think to wave at someone."

Sam tried a subtle smile. Actually, I'm not sure who I waved at. I thought someone waved at me, but now I think it was a tree limb moving in the breeze."

"What breeze?"

"The one over there." Sam indicated a sweep of forest. "It was strong for a moment. It fooled me." She hesitated, seeing suspicion in Heather's eyes and wondering why it was there. "Or maybe it really was someone."

"What were they wearing?"

"Something greenish," Sam said, doing her best to sound bored. "If it was a real person, that is."

"Male or female?"

Sam shrugged. "Who knows? Probably it wasn't a person at all." She paused, grinned. "Maybe it was the Greenbriar Ghost."

Heather's eyes widened, then hardened back down as she scanned the forest boundaries.

"I was joking," Sam chided. "You don't believe that ghost nonsense, do you?"

"The Forest Knight isn't something to joke about."

"You call it the Forest Knight? That's sort of an old-fashioned term."

Heather eyed her. That wasn't a pleasant sensation. "It's not old-fashioned. It's respectful." Now she paused and plastered on a grimace of a smile. "The Forest Knight is part of Greenbriar University history and lore, and that makes him part of Gamma history. That deserves some respect, don't you think?"

"Sure," Sam agreed. "I'm sorry if I offended you."

"You didn't. I should apologize for being so bitchy."

"Is your stomach virus still bothering you?"

"Yes," Heather said, a faint foul scent rising to agree. "Several of the squad members have it." She eyed Sam.

"I'm so sorry. It must be miserable, especially with a game tonight." Sam exuded all the pity she could muster. "Did you ask Mildred about it? Is it food poisoning?"

"Probably. Mildred threw out all the leftovers in the fridge just to be safe." She paused, her eyes hard on Sam's. "We all got the curse this morning too."

Knowing she was looking for a reaction, unsure why, Sam nodded and spoke blandly. "I think that's common, isn't it? Women who live together often cycle together. Or so I've read."

Heather, her eyes scanning the forest, nodded dismissively.

Sam walked into the house, knowing she'd passed some sort of test, unsure of what it was. Then, as she started up the grand staircase, her own thoughts came back to haunt her. *Is Merilynn dead? Did I see her ghost?*

The Stone in the
Sword

13

In the forest, or perhaps in the lake, drifting along the dappled sunlit paths, Merilynn thought she might be dreaming. She hoped she was still in the dream that had begun so many hours ago. *Has it really been that long?*

Dreamtime was not the same thing as waking time. Not the same thing at all. That could very well mean she had been asleep for endless minutes, not hours.

Or maybe I'm awake.

Maybe I'm dead.

That thought panicked her and she tried to push to the surface, to emerge into wakefulness and feel her bed beneath her body, her head nestled safely into her soft down pillow, which was covered with a cobalt case printed with golden stars and silver moons.

Kendra! she thought as hard as she could. *Help me wake up!*

Slowly, as if swimming through thick, cool water, she felt herself moving forward. In the distance, she saw a spot of light. *Swim to it,* she told herself. She stroked her arms forward and back and kicked her feet, hoping the movement would translate into thrashing that would wake up Kendra, who would, in turn, help her to awaken, to find her way back from the long, long dream.

Kendra!

The light grew brighter and she became more aware of the woods than the lake. She recognized Applehead Forest as she moved through it, faster and faster. Suddenly, full daylight shone on her. She saw the road beneath her, just for an instant, and then she was back in the forest again, still heading in the same direction. Toward Gamma House.

Kendra! She concentrated on the word, willing herself to say it aloud so that her roommate would hear her. The forest flashed by, more daylight gleamed ahead of her, growing quickly. I'm almost awake! *I'm almost out of the woods!*

She laughed as she sped toward the forest's edge, delighting in the dream for an instant, then worrying again. *What if I just keep going?*

Nearing the last few trees, she forced herself to slow down and step out from among them as if she were awake. *Kendra?* she called. *Where are you?*

There was Gamma House. As she emerged into daylight and stepped onto the lawn, she could see it with the clarity of a dream, all the details, even some peeling paint she had never noticed before, on the lower left side of the veranda railing.

There was one girl visible. Merilynn tried to move across the lawn, to see who it was, but she couldn't move out of the forest. *Great. Just great. Sleep paralysis. Come on, wake up!*

Her body wouldn't obey, so she concentrated her energy on seeing the lone woman on the veranda. The figure turned slightly and Merilynn knew her.

Samantha! she called as loud as she could. *Samantha.*

Sam turned and looked. Merilynn called again and raised her hand, waving at her.

Samantha saw her. She waved back.

Then another figure came out of the house and saw Sam's raised hand, started to follow Sam's gaze.

Merilynn, all instinct, instantly let herself be drawn back among the trees, out of sight. *Out of danger.*

14

Kendra!

"Merilynn!" Kendra awoke abruptly from her catnap, positive she'd heard her roommate calling her, not just once, but several times. *She was trying to wake me up!*

Kendra sat up so rapidly that the room briefly spun, but an instant later she was on her feet, searching the room. "Merilynn?" she asked, before opening a closet door. "I know you're here. You can't scare me by popping out and saying boo!" She yanked open the closet door, knowing the girl would be there.

But she wasn't. *Maybe I dreamed it.*

Kendra!

This time, she knew it was no dream. "Where the heck are you?" she said, checking inside the other closet without fanfare. Merilynn was in the room; she could tell by the closeness of her voice. "I've been so worried about you," Kendra said as she looked under one bed, then the other. Under the desks.

Kendra!

The voice was in her ear, right in her ear! Kendra stood still, listening, waiting, and for one or two seconds, fear prickled across her belly and down her back. Then she realized that her roommate had to be outside the door, in the hall.

Smiling to herself, Kendra tiptoed to the door, paused, then yanked it open.

Sam Penrose, hand raised in a fist, stared at her, goggle-eyed.

"What are you doing?" they both asked in panicked voices.

Sam recovered first. "I was about to knock."

"Christ, get *in* here." Kendra stood back to allow Sam inside, then shut the door firmly and turned to look at her. "I swear, I thought you were about to punch me. You scared the hell out of me!"

"How?"

"I thought you were Merilynn. I swear, Sam, I heard her. I heard her *in this room*. In my ear. Not more than a minute ago."

"You did?" Sam shook her head. "I heard her too."

"Was she calling my name?"

"No. She called *my* name. Outside. Hey, are you sure this room is clean?"

"Why? Do you smell something?"

Sam rolled her eyes. "I mean *clean*. No bugs?"

"Bugs? I hope not. Why are you asking about that when Merilynn needs—"

"*Electronic* bugs," Sam interrupted, almost whispering.

Kendra felt foolish. *I should have known that.* Instead of speaking, she shrugged in reply, then watched as Sam went over the room, peering at every inch of it, running her fingers beneath the desks and beds.

"I think we're okay," she said finally, still speaking very softly. She sat down on Kendra's bed and patted the spot next to her.

"How could you have heard her outside when I heard her in here?" Kendra asked quietly as soon as she was seated.

Sam shook her head. "I don't know. Maybe it's a trick."

"Merilynn's trick, or someone else's?"

"I don't know." Sam paused. "There's more."

"What?"

Sam leaned closer and whispered, "I saw her."

"Where?" Kendra controlled her excitement. "When?"

"Just a couple minutes ago, by the woods."

"We should go get her. She's probably using telepathy to call us."

Sam touched her hand. "Listen, it might be bad."

"What do you mean? What did you see?"

"I saw her, but she was too far away to hear."

"Then it had to be telepathy."

"Maybe. I hope so. Kendra, she may be dead. I saw an apparition."

"How do you know?"

"She vanished right in front of my eyes." Sam looked at the ceiling. "I heard her first. I looked around, thinking she was on the porch, hiding—"

"Like I thought she was in this room with me."

"Yes. But when I finally saw her, she was way across the lawn. I think she knew that I saw her—

that's when she waved. I waved back and she just sort of dematerialized or something. I don't know how to describe it."

"You're sure she didn't just step back behind a tree?"

Sam made a face. "I know what I saw, even if I don't know what it really was, and Merilynn's image disappeared as soon as Heather came up behind me."

Kendra nodded. "That makes sense."

"It does?"

"Of course." She leaned to Sam's ear and whispered, "You asked me before if I knew about the secret society?"

Sam nodded. "How much do you know?"

"I know that it's real. I know it's existed since the sorority was founded. I know there's a whole lot more going on in that east wing than drinking and sex."

"Do you know the name?"

This time, Kendra nodded. "Do you?"

"Yes."

"Don't say it."

"I won't."

The girls looked at each other and embarrassed smiles appeared. "If we say the name three times," Kendra said, "the society will appear in front of us and we won't be able to get rid of them."

Sam smiled. "You think Heather's one of them?"

"Undoubtedly. There should be thirteen altogether."

"Your source?"

"My family. Generations. What's yours?"

"Research." Sam hesitated. "So what do you think? Is Merilynn alive? Or did I see a ghost?"

Kendra thought a moment, then asked, "What was she wearing?"

"Something long and lavender."

"That's not what she wore to bed. Did she look . . . well, wet or anything?"

"Like Holly, you mean?"

Kendra nodded. "When we saw Holly last night, she was just like you described. Long white dress, all wet, her hair was wet. And Eve was wearing what she had on the last time I saw her."

"Well, that's interesting, but it's not proof she's alive," Sam said. She could have been put into other clothes and then . . ."

"Killed?"

Sam nodded.

"How did she look? I mean, what was your general impression of her?"

"I don't understand."

"Well, when you saw Holly, what was your reaction?"

"I thought she was dead."

"She looked pretty dead to me last night too, even when I heard her voice. Eve didn't have the same— I don't know—energy? Yes. Energy. Her energy wasn't the same as it was when she was alive. It was subdued, a little sad." She rubbed her chin. "Very sad. Not like Evie at all." Kendra fell silent and waited for Sam to speak.

"She was very far away, but my impression was that it was her. Her energy. That sounds peculiar."

"Don't analyze. I know what you mean, and you know I know."

Sam's mouth crooked in a shadow of a one-sided

smile. "Yeah. Well, then, I'll go out on a limb. This is just feelings though, no facts."

Kendra rolled her eyes. "I know. Now tell me what you felt."

"There was a sort of fairy-tale feel to her. I think it was because of what she was wearing. I don't know if it was a long dress or a cloak, it was much too far away to tell, but it had kind of a 'Glenda, Good Witch of the West' feel. From *The Wizard of Oz*. But less lace."

"I know."

"If I had to guess—this is so illogical."

"Don't Spock me, Sam. Just say what you felt."

"I think you were right about the telepathy. I think maybe I saw her as she wanted to be seen."

"A purple cloak," Kendra said thoughtfully.

"Lavender. And I'm not sure it was a cloak."

"Shhh. It doesn't matter. Purple, and lavender is a shade of purple, is a sorcerer's color. It's associated with magic and wizards and witches. Merilynn has an entire set of herbs and potions and crystals. She's into magic. Did you know that?"

"Well, I'm not surprised. After that performance with the tires and calling the deer . . ."

"And every cheerleader is on the rag," Kendra said. "I checked. Except Michele. She's not here at all, as far as I can tell. Sam," she said after a moment of silence, "I wish I could remember better what I heard last night, but I think maybe Merilynn is all right. That she went off on her own."

"An adventure," Sam said. "Like we talked about in the first place."

"Yeah, but I think something's gone wrong. She's trying to call us."

"Any idea where she might be?"

Kendra nodded, her heart thudding. "Out there. In the forest. Maybe at the chapel."

"She wanted to go last night."

"I said I'd go with her today and she was fine with that," Kendra said. "But maybe she went alone anyway. And something happened. Something to do with what Holly Gayle said." She paused, trying to sort jumbled memories of the night before. There was the warning about the sorceress and her familiar— Kendra was pretty sure that had to be Malory and, most likely, Brittany, and reminded Sam. "But," she added, "I still don't think they're involved in Merilynn's disappearance."

"Why?"

"It just doesn't *feel* like they are. Sam, I really think she went off on her own to help Holly and Eve. Damn it, I wish I could remember more. The thing is, I think Merilynn might be trapped somewhere out there. Maybe the chapel, maybe even on the island."

"Holly almost lured me into the water." Sam stood up and looked out the window. "There's not much daylight left. I don't think we could even get to the chapel and back before dark. I'm sure we couldn't. And the island is impossible."

"We have to go to the chapel." Kendra stood next to Sam and watched shiny crows working the back lawn for their supper. She shivered.

"Too dangerous," Sam declared.

"I think it's safe tonight."

"You do? Why?"

"Most of the—society—will be at the football game. Cheering and popping Midol. Malory's been

dragging herself around all afternoon moaning
about food poisoning. And she's not the only one.
Most of them are miserable. Brittany's the only one
who's not looking a little green." Kendra studied
Sam. "You know what that means, don't you?"

"Tell me."

"If Merilynn can put hexes on *them,* she's one
powerful little sorceress herself."

15

"Where the hell is my football player?"

Coach Max Choad, accompanied by a small but voluptuous Latina coed, appeared in the kitchen doorway of Gamma House, full of piss and bluster, and stared furiously at Heather, Malory, Brittany, and several of the J-clones. The cheerleaders all held glasses of freshly made purple pick-me-up, having a well-needed jolt before the game.

"I asked you girls a question." The girl with him hovered just behind him, looking anxious, but exuding anger as well. Heather didn't recognize her. "Answer me." Choad adjusted his stance to a wide-legged immovable-soldier look, hands on hips, in an imitation of a peacock showing its colors. It worked pretty well, with his military haircut and heavy ridge of brow. The gray sweats weren't as effective as cammie fatigues might have been, but all in all, Heather thought, not too shabby.

Mildred McArthur appeared from the recesses of the kitchen, a new pitcher of her magic potion in hand. Like a big gray army tank, she rolled toward the table where her girls sat, put down the pitcher, and folded her arms across her chest. She was every inch as macho as Coach Choad and while he didn't back down under her steely tight-bunned stare, he did look a little more respectful. The coed gave off noticeably less anger.

Mildred placed herself behind Heather Horner, like a loyal mastiff. You could almost hear her snarling, though she didn't say a word.

Heather, who had felt like absolute, total crap all day, appreciated the housekeeper's presence. They all did, of course, but Heather was Mildred's pet, and she knew it. Between the housekeeper's wonderful purple juice, which she'd added something extra to to help ease the gas problems and female problems—she wouldn't say what, but who cared?—and her huge rock-slab presence, Heather felt some of her spunk returning. She could handle this, just like the Fatas had agreed she would, earlier in the day.

She stood up, knowing how good her body looked in the uniform, using it, and met Choad's beady gaze. *"Your* football player took *our* best cheerleader and ran off," she told him. "You know Malory Thomas, our president?" she added. Without waiting for a reply, she held her hand out and Malory produced a pale pink envelope, took out a folded note on matching stationery, and silently handed it to Heather. "If you think you're any more upset than we are," she said, "you're wrong. Duane Hieman took advantage of Michele. And now they're gone." She unfolded the note.

"Duane and I are engaged," the dark-haired coed with Choad said. "He wouldn't cheat on me."

"If you believe that," Brittany chirped, "you don't know men."

"'Dear Sisters,'" Heather read, ignoring the girl, "'I'm sorry I won't be there for the game tonight, but Duane Hieman and I are in love. He's the most wonderful man I've ever met and he's asked me to go away with him. I'm carrying his child and we want to keep it. Please don't look for us. Once we're settled, I'll be in touch. Gamma rules! Love, Your Sister, Michele Marano.'" She held the note out.

Choad snatched it, glanced at it, passed it to the football jock's wronged fiancée. "My boys said they went drinking with some of you last night," he grumbled. "Duane was with them. They said you and some of your sluts here seduced them."

Malory laughed. Not a nice sound. Then she locked her gaze on Choad. "Your boys can't resist pussy, so they're blaming their lack of control on *my* girls?"

Silence filled the room. Heather could see the concentration on Malory's face. She was doing something to the coach, whose look of resolve began to crumble.

"Don't your boys have any discipline?" Malory asked softly.

Choad looked slightly befuddled. Heather zoomed in. "Look, Coach, a few of us did have a couple beers with a few of your players, but that's all. We weren't out long."

"Where did you go to get drunk?" the coed asked.

"Just out on the lawn, not far from here. We took a blanket and sat on the ground. It was cold, so we weren't even out long—and we certainly didn't get drunk." She paused. "Michele and Duane were with us. They stayed behind when the rest of us returned to our houses."

"We returned to Gamma," Malory added. "Heather, Brittany, and I returned. We assume that your star quarterback and—who were the other ones?"

"Spencer Lake and Perry Seville," Heather said.

Malory nodded. "I'll vouch for what Heather just told you." She put her chin up. "I assure you, one of your jocks is not what I'd look for if I wanted to get laid."

Brittany wrinkled her nose. "Me either.'"

"We just wanted to relax," Heather finished. Being a cheerleader, she didn't dare claim disinterest in laying jocks. It wouldn't have rung true. "Maybe we can figure this out. What did your boys tell you?"

"Not much. They were drunk off their asses and full of nonsense about getting lost in the woods."

"It wasn't with us," Heather said, glancing at Brittany, who gave her a tiny nod of approval. "We were sitting near the woods, but none of us would ever go into them at night."

"Bull," Choad said. "You kids go into the woods to make out."

"Talk about an urban legend," Malory said. "That's the real bull. One of our cheerleaders died in the woods just before school started. All they found was bones. Surely you remember that, Coach Choad?"

"Of course I do. What's that got to do with it?"

"We like our skins," Brittany said. "We wouldn't risk losing them."

"Look," Heather said, "I don't know what your

boys did. They *said* they were going back to their house. They took off and so did we. Only Michele and Duane stayed behind."

"If I had to guess," Malory said, sounding bored, "I'd say your boys got some more beer, got shit-faced, and maybe really did get lost in the woods."

Heather nodded. She barely remembered what happened, but she did remember that Art Caliburn had rescued her and brought her back to Gamma before Brittany messed up the players' memories. Choad didn't say anything about Art in particular, so Brittany's spell must have done what it was supposed to. Art was sweet; Heather was sorry he didn't remember his heroic deeds.

"Duane and I are getting married," the coed reminded them.

"I doubt it, sweetie," Malory said dismissively. "He's been planting his seeds in another garden. Why don't you try to snatch yourself another jock? You know how to snatch, don't you?"

The coed stared at her.

"You just open your lips and blow."

The coed and the coach turned and stomped off. Instantly Malory laughed. "Did you see the look on that girl's face?"

"Malory, you shouldn't have said that," Brittany said. "It made you sound slutty."

"Oh, who cares?"

"Sit, Heather," Mildred rumbled. "I'll pour you all some more juice."

Heather gratefully did as she was told. Mildred filled her glass first and she drank greedily, made a slight face. "It's a little tart," she said.

"Just like you," Malory drawled, waving Mildred off. "No, thanks, Mildred. I'll stick to lemon juice."

"This will fix your stomach."

"No, I'll be fine."

"It really works," Heather said, halfway through her glass.

Brittany giggled, and pushed away from the table. "Excuse me, ladies. I have to pee."

16

The cheerleaders, full of juice and moaning less about their periodic problems, took off for the football stadium half an hour later. Malory and Brittany left the kitchen and walked out onto the veranda to enjoy the last of the daylight. The woods cast early pretwilight shadows that beckoned to Brittany. She longed for a romp.

"Thank you for overseeing the burial this morning," Malory said, sounding relaxed for the first time that day.

"Jenny and Ginny did just fine."

"No cases of vapors?"

"No freaking out," Brittany corrected. "Keep your language up to date."

"Don't be bitchy. You know what I mean."

"Ginny freaked out once."

Malory turned. "Tell me."

"It wasn't about the bodies. She doesn't like chipmunks."

"What did you do?"

"Offered her a piece of candy. The bitch said I was a disgusting rodent. So I bit her."

"You bit her?" Mal laughed.

"No blood. I was careful. Jenny's much nicer." Brittany, leaning against the veranda railing, stared at the woods. "They're the real thing. Real Fata Morgana material. Jenny for sure. Ginny, probably."

"That's good. We've had so few that last lately. They either get themselves killed or they prove unworthy." Malory paused. "So, what do you think of Nancy? Do you think we're rushing things, initiating her tonight?"

"I think she's a good temporary answer to our problem," Brittany said. "We may have to do a little binding spell on her temper though. We can't have her running around killing people every time she's got PMS."

"I agree." Malory paused. "Sorry."

A stench wafted into Brittany's pert nose. "I hope you're not going to take that ass over to Professor Tongue's tonight. You'd kill him."

Malory smiled. "I could test his love for me."

"He'd pass out. Why don't you break down and have some of Mildred's juice? I noticed a distinct lessening of stink after that last batch."

"You and your magical urine. Sorry, love, I don't drink pee. Not even yours."

"Why not? You'll drink anything else."

"Back when my brother was still alive and I was just a sorcerer's apprentice—" She paused. "Actually, I was a quick study. I was at journeyman level. In fact, it was only a year or two before I trapped my old teacher and took his power and added it to my own."

"I know the story. Tell me why you won't drink urine."

"My mentor gave me a potion once, when I became ill after eating some bad rabbit. It was food poisoning and I was much sicker than I've been today, vomiting, shitting blood, you know, the whole E-coli thing."

Brittany nodded, pleased to hear a new story, no matter how crude.

"Myrddin was a great teacher and sorceror, but he made his share of mistakes. Once, he tried to create a strange creature—"

"The platypus. You've told me that story hundreds, maybe thousands of times."

Malory laughed. "Very well. My mentor created a concoction to cure me, but it nearly killed me. I thought I'd vomit my innards out before it wore off. The ingredient was the urine of one of Myrddin's familiars."

"Anyone I know?"

"I doubt it; this was in the old country."

"We travel."

"Do you know any badgers?"

"No. I know a raccoon from Bavaria. He's famous. He inspired a Beatles song."

"You're such a name-dropper."

Brittany took a packet of sunflower seeds from the change pocket on her jeans and ripped it open with her teeth. "Are you allergic to badger urine?"

"The urine of a familiar is an old cure and energizer for humans. But I was like Myrrdin. My mother was human, but my father was the Wild Man of the Woods." She paused. "That's what we called the local nature diety back then."

"I know all that."

"Those such as Myrrdin and I cannot drink the urine of a familiar. I lived only because of my human nature."

"I thought you just had a thing about drinking urine."

"No."

"Why have you never told me this before?"

"It never came up."

"And why didn't Myrrdin know this?"

"Our kind are few and his teacher did not know. So how could he? It's rare for one of us to become ill. Very rare. There was no reason for him to know it until, experimenting to find out what had happened, he ingested a tiny amount himself and had the same reaction, though milder. He'd taken in less and he was more powerful than I was then, so it only took him a few days to recover. It took me months."

"You're easily as strong as your teacher was."

"Yes. But I still wouldn't want to experience even a fraction of that agony again." She paused. "If I had my athame, it probably couldn't touch me at all."

They silently watched distant figures of students moving about the campus. A breeze full of autumn promise and chimney smoke beguiled Brittany's nose. "All Hallow's Eve draws near. We need to decide on a sacrifice worthy of the Forest Knight. And we must find more women worthy of becoming Fata Morgana before then."

"Merilynn," Malory said softly, "will be the sacrifice. I've decided."

"She's missing."

"I know. Of all the daughters I've born over the

centuries, she is the finest. I believe she has great power and I hoped we could make her one of our own. But her will is too strong and she's under the influence of Holly Gayle. I believe she does her bidding."

"We should find her as quickly as we can."

"Yes. But we have to watch her. I suspect she knows about the athame."

"Why do you believe that?"

"I think Holly Gayle was here for her last night. She already has Eve Camlan. She's after Merilynn. She's gathering souls who can help her get free. If Merilynn is looking for my stone, she may have enough power to use it on Holly's behalf. Against me."

"Why do you think she has so much power? You've seen no proof. I think you're just swayed by her eyes. They're her father's eyes."

"They're the eyes of *both* her fathers. No other daughter has had so much of the Forest Knight in her."

"The priest is not entirely human?"

"No. He carries the blood of the Forest Knight. His mother was a student here many years ago. We were here part of the time she was here—a beauty, entirely human, but with a fey quality that appealed to me. To us. Do you remember her?"

Brittany shook her head. "No."

"She had auburn hair like Merilynn's and blue eyes. We tried to interest her in Gamma but she didn't take the bait."

Brittany searched her memory. "There have been so many."

"Her name was Gwen Aldan."

"I remember that one. She left school. She was pregnant."

"Um-hmm. She was dating a frat boy that I was interested in trying out. I don't even remember his name, just that he was faithful to her. It was very annoying." She smiled like a contented cat. "He didn't marry her though. He didn't know about the baby. I had him a year later, but he was a Johnny-come-early. Not worth much in bed."

"I don't remember much about him. Other than he existed."

"He wasn't worth remembering. I only tried him once and you weren't there. I doubt I even mentioned him to you."

"How did her baby come to have the knight's blood in him?"

"You don't remember that?" Mal rubbed her chin. "I think you were off on that lesbian kick at the time. I was pretty annoyed about that."

"Sure." Brittany smiled as visions of a tall Nordic blond student with long legs and full lips came into her mind. "I remember that pissed you off, so I didn't tell you, but Gretchen was a cross-dresser. She was a he."

"You little twat. Why did you want to anger me?"

"It made me feel loved. I knew you needed me. And you're an incredible lover when you're jealous."

"That's sweet. Remind me to spank you later."

Brittany grinned. "I will, just as soon as you stop stinking up the place."

"Bitch," Malory said affectionately. "One night, during your fling, Gwen Aldan and her quick-draw boyfriend decided to go into the woods. I followed them, primarily because there was a full moon and spring had come early. The sap was running and the Green Knight was very active that year, just before the equinox. I was horny, nearly as much as he, I think. I had some vague plan to cast a glamour and join them in a threesome.

"They wandered farther into the woods than I expected, across Applehead Road, and straight for the Knight's Chapel. That excited me even more. Humans don't venture there on their own, no matter the stories—"

"Don't tell me what I already know. Tell me what happened."

"You are so impatient, one would think you didn't have all the time in the world." Malory leaned forward and took a deep breath. "I love autumn." She looked at Brittany, smiled at her instant of patience, then continued. "Gwen and her beau made it to the clearing, then hesitated. I knew they felt the power there. Not to mention our protection spells. They had to be frightened. The boy certainly was. I heard him telling her they should go elsewhere. He said others might catch them in the act.

"But Gwen was adamant. I think his fear just turned her on. I also think she could sense the influence of the knight and it excited her. She began kissing and fondling the boy as they stood in the clearing. He started to respond. I sensed the knight's presence and kept hidden in the trees.

"Gwen undressed and stood naked in the moonlight in the clearing. The grass was new and tender, the oak leaves bright and fresh. She was beautiful, irresistible to the human and to the knight. The boy undressed and lay on top of her." She paused. "I should have known he was boring then, just going straight for the missionary position."

"Did they hear the knight?"

"He wasn't like he was last night. The humans were in love, even if they were bad at lovemaking. The knight approves of love, the old softie."

"And they weren't actually defiling his chapel," Brittany added.

"Even if they'd been in there, it was not defilement. It was nothing like the idiotic orgy we had last night. *That* was defiling the chapel."

"Tell me about it. I can't believe I let you do that."

"You couldn't stop me. You indulge me, little one. You know that."

Brittany let her hand move onto Malory's, squeezed it.

"The knight arrived that night in a gentle whirlwind that whistled softly through the trees and bushes. Just as the boy entered Gwen, the knight took form—I could see him, though they couldn't, of course. But from the sounds Gwen made as the knight entered the boy's body, I'd say she sensed the passion.

"Oh, Britt, it was a sight to see. No wonder I assumed the boy was worth fucking. Once the knight possessed him, he became more lover than Gwen had ever imagined. He was magnificent, and his excitement spread in waves through the clearing, entering the forest. His passion was so great that I was overcome with orgasms and fell to the ground, unable to stand. But I watched. Finally, it was over. The Forest Knight, having sown his seed, departed.

"The couple slept deeply. I walked around them,

sat by them, touched them. They never knew. But I knew the knight had impregnated Gwen, so I kept track of her and then her child."

"But it was a boy."

"It was the priest, one-third elemental, two-thirds human. Males partly fathered by forest gods are rarely born, and if they are, they rarely live long. But this one thrived. Gwen married Douglas Morris, a schoolteacher, before the child was born, so the infant was christened Martin Morris. He showed no signs of his elemental roots, except for his eyes, but I had the Fatas here keep an eye on him anyway. They told me he was handsome and charismatic but lacked any traits of the Forest Knight."

"That's to be expected," Brittany said.

"So it is. I still thought to make him my lover to help sire my next daughter, just to see what would happen, but I didn't get around to it until the Fatas reported that he'd become a priest, denying the lust that had to be in his nature."

"You and priests," Brittany chided.

"Forbidden fruit is always the tastiest."

Brittany grinned. "So Martin Morris must have been the cherry on your sundae."

"Mmmm. That man was delicious and he resisted me as no mere human male ever could. I'd never admit this to anyone but you, but I actually had to cast a glamour to get him to make love to me."

"Mal, you do that all the time."

"To speed things up. When I want a real lover, a father for my child, I prefer to seduce him the old-fashioned way. I brought him to the chapel without magick; the priest wanted to see it. In fact, he'd been there before. Quite the scholar on the occult."

"A natural interest."

Mal smiled. "Yes. I impressed him with stories of the Forest Knight and when I saw desire in his eyes, I tried to seduce him. I nearly had him, but the damned Papist had a will of iron. Finally, I cast a little light glamour and his will of iron turned into a willy of iron." She laughed like a young girl.

"Once I had him where I wanted him, I removed the spell. He couldn't deny me at that point. From that union, I created Merilynn. That is why I believe she's so powerful. Not as powerful as I am, of course."

"Malory," Brittany ventured, "you had him impregnate you at the chapel."

"I enjoy it more that way."

"I know. May I ask you something?"

"Of course."

"Did you sense the Forest Knight?"

"I always sense the knight."

"I know, but I mean in the same way you did when you peeped the priest's conception."

"Peeped?"

"You know what I mean."

Malory hesitated. "As the daughter of a Green Man myself, I have a similar degree of lust. Making love in the chapel makes me one with the Forest Knight. I am the same."

"Almost the same. I just want to know if he manifested. If he rode you or the priest."

"He didn't possess the priest," Malory said. "I would have known if he had."

"Could he have been in you?"

"My lust is the same as his."

"Mal, what I'm saying is, if he rode with you,

Merilynn might be more elemental than you think. She could be *as powerful as you.*"

"Nonsense."

"I hope so."

"Why would you think that?"

"You've been too ill to think about it, but some-body is behind everything that happened today. The gas. Did you notice, every senior sister had gas? No juniors, sophomores, or freshman. Just seniors."

"Coincidence," Malory said without too much certainty.

"No. Because the girls who all got their periods this morning? Every single one was a cheerleader. Every one of them had problems with stickless wings or broken tampon strings. I asked around. *Every single one.* No exceptions. And the senior cheerleaders like Heather have *all* the problems." She squeezed her mistress's hand. "That's why *I* think you're right about Merilynn. Especially now that you've told me this story. She must have done it."

"Not bad, huh?" Malory said with pride.

"Not bad? She even got *you!* You yourself said you don't get sick easily. If she's strong enough to cast a glamour over you, then she may be your equal or more."

"No, that's just ridiculous. I wasn't on my guard. I had too much to drink and my human nature got the upper hand, that's all."

"I hope so."

"Besides, even if it were true, she was raised by a priest with more morals than an inner-directed atheist."

"That's a lot of morals. Religious nuts are usually so easily bought and sold."

"The priest is no religious nut. He may not even be into dogma, but he has the spiritual streak. I suspect he thrives on the discipline of his profession. And he's a scholar."

"A martyr?"

"I'd say no, judging by Merilynn's behavior."

"Then why did you let him raise her?"

"Honestly? I almost always leave the girls with their fathers. You know I've used men of various cloths plenty of times. Not the average preacher, mind you, but the fiery ones. I choose them for their dogmatic attitudes, the stronger the better." She chuckled. "They're *so* easy to seduce. And they make lousy parents because they're usually too strict and shove so much religion down the girls' throats that they're primed to rebel."

Whenever Malory decided to produce a new daughter, Brittany bore it without pointing out that the daughters rarely lived long after Malory brought them into the sisterhood. She didn't point it out now. Instead, she said, "So, you overlooked this priest's morals and intellect because of his heritage?"

"Wouldn't you?"

"Yes. Now. What are we going to do about your daughter?"

"We have to find out where she is and watch her until she leads us to my stone. Then . . . we lock her up tight and save her for All Hallow's Eve."

Behind them, someone pushed one of the front doors open. Brittany turned, then Malory. "Hi, Samantha, Kendra."

"Hello," they both said.

"Off to the game?" Brittany asked, looking at the knapsacks both carried.

"No," Sam said, boldly swinging hers around and patting it. "We're off to study."

"On a Friday night?" Mal asked.

"We're nerds," Kendra said, smiling. "What can we say?"

"I may come by the library later myself," Malory replied. "See you there?"

"No," Sam said. "We're actually going down to Caledonia to study."

"We're going to my granny's house," Kendra added. "She's making us a home-cooked dinner. We're going to study there."

"That's a strange place to study," Brittany chirped around a sunflower seed.

"Not really," Sam said without a trace of defensiveness. "We're working a report together for Professor McCobb's cultural iconography class. We're doing a paper on local lore, and Kendra's grandmother is an expert."

"She worked here, didn't she?"

Kendra smiled. "Malory, I'm surprised you'd remember that. Yes, she did, but that's not really important. It's the stories that were handed down to her about the Greenbriar Ghost and the Puckwudgies that we're interested in."

"That sounds like something your roommate, Merilynn, would be interested in," Malory replied. "Why isn't she with you?"

"She's not in the class," Sam said.

"But it seems strange she wouldn't tag along. I know how much she likes that kind of thing."

"She's busy," Sam said.

"Oh? Big date?"

"I don't know for sure. Maybe she's going to her

father's. Maybe to see friends. I didn't ask, she didn't tell me."

"When was this?" Malory asked casually. "I've been in the house all day and I haven't run into her once."

"I saw her earlier this afternoon, but just for a moment. She was in a hurry to take off."

Malory nodded. "Well, have fun, you guys."

"Don't drink and drive," Brittany called after them.

Exchanging glances, they both turned to watch the freshman duo walk quickly toward the nearest parking lot. A moment later, exchanging glances when Sam Penrose's white Camry drove slowly by, Sam waved, Kendra too.

Brittany raised her hand. "Well, I didn't really think we'd see a car. I didn't think they were really going to Caledonia, at least not to eat dinner with an old lady."

"I still don't think they are," Malory said. "If they're really going down to Granny's house, who cares?"

"Maybe they're pumping her for information."

"Britt, they *admitted* that. And who cares? Now, be a love and race over to the woods. To the chapel. Make sure nothing's been disturbed, just in case that's where they're really headed."

"We need to go there together to do the quick-rot spell on those corpses Jenny and Ginny buried. If we transport ourselves via aport, we can get it done before they get there, even if they're on their way."

"Brittany, that takes energy I don't have today. That's why I want you to go by yourself. If they show up, watch them. Follow them. They might be looking for her, or they might know where she is. I wouldn't be surprised if they're taking her food."

"Okay." Brittany stood straight and stretched. "When Samantha claimed she saw Merilynn today, did you think it was a lie?"

"I—no. But I still don't believe it. The girl is gone. Samantha is an amazingly accomplished liar."

"I think she was telling the truth," Brittany said firmly. "Granted, she's difficult to read most of the time, but when humans make an absolute statement, I can tell if they're lying or not. I don't believe she was."

Malory nodded. "Okay, she saw her. Now scoot! You need to get to the chapel quickly."

Brittany handed Malory the almost-empty sunflower seed bag, glanced around, saw no one, transformed into her elemental form, and joyously sped into the forest.

17

Father Martin Morris sat alone on the comfortable old couch in the cozy living room of the little California bungalow-style house he'd lived in ever since he'd taken over Caledonia's little parish more than twenty years ago. The room was lit by only by one lamp on a side table and the television, which was airing the 7:00 P.M. rerun of the previous night's *Late Night with Conan O'Brien*, one of Martin's favorite guilty pleasures.

Merilynn's too. Before the show had started rerunning on Comedy Central, before Merilynn had gone off to college, they had taped it nearly every night and watched it during supper.

Tonight, he was all alone, except for Pio, his aging fat tabby who was snoring away on the back of the couch. Delores, his live-in housekeeper and Merilynn's mother substitute, had been living-in less and less lately. After all these years, at fifty-two, she had finally found romance. Of course, she'd never gone looking when Merilynn was home. Now, Martin expected Delores would announce wedding plans soon, and he was happy for her, but very sorry for himself. He would miss her company, though not half as much as he already missed Merilynn's. *A priest suffering from empty nest syndrome. There's something novel.*

In a perfect world, Merilynn would be here beside him, watching Conan dismember politicians and going off on ridiculous tangents like a big Irish Robin Williams whenever a guest turned into a snore-fest. *Snorefest.* That was Merilynn's term. *Good God, how I miss her!*

Tonight, if she were here, and Delores was out, he would have zapped two Hungry Man Salisbury Steak TV dinners instead of one, and they would have eaten every last bite (except for the generous pieces of meat they always cut up for Pio). They'd bond over the damned dinners, telling one another how disapproving Delores would be if she knew. And that simple thing, a silly secret kept, had seemed grand to little Merilynn, and truth be told, to him as well.

Instead, there was one empty-compartmented TV dinner tray and a fork, on the coffee table. Thanks to Pio, there wasn't a drop of evidence left (or there wouldn't be, once he tossed the dinner tray and rinsed the fork). He smiled. The cardboard tray was clean enough to put in the recycle bin, but he'd bury it in the trash so that Delores wouldn't be so likely to deliver a lecture about chemical preservatives or look hurt that he hadn't eaten the bland little shepherd's pie she'd made for him. The pie, more evidence, would disappear soon too, chopped up and put out on old plastic plates, a special treat for the small colony of feral cats he cared for.

Settling back, he put his feet on the table. Pio opened one sleepy eye, then oozed his gray and black tiger-stripes down the back of the couch and across the seat, then onto Martin's lap. The feline began purring and pressing his paws up and down on the priest's thigh. Martin endured the sharp claws—Merilynn liked to say that their Pio caused stigmata, instead of enduring them like his holy namesake.

And she was right.

Merilynn, I wish you'd call me. Absently, he stroked the cat and tried to concentrate on Conan, but found himself glancing at the Regulator pendulum wall clock and wondering what his little girl was up to. He did that a lot, but more than usual since this noon or so. Generally she phoned for a moment or two every day, and usually warned him when she wouldn't be able to, but he hadn't heard from her since Wednesday. It hadn't been long, and it was a Friday night. *Maybe she went to a football game.*

The thought amused him so much that he chuckled. Pio gave him a disapproving glare.

On-screen, Conan was making throaty meows and raising his eyebrows suggestively to cover for a boring starlet whose breasts were engineering marvels and probably had higher IQs than her brain. He studied her. *Is she drunk? High? Simply stupid or terribly nervous? Who cares? What's Merilynn doing?* He smiled again. He knew his girl; she wouldn't be at a football game, but otherwise, all bets were off.

Conan smoothed his eyebrows, cutting up the actress's drone with manic double entendres, but Martin barely heard them. Merilynn was smart, but she was impulsive too, and he could never completely stop worrying about her. She needed someone to ground her and he had been relieved when she told him that she had reconnected with a down-to-earth girl named Sam whom she'd met at camp and never forgotten. Back then, she'd called the girl "the funnest party pooper" she'd ever met. He had sensed a little bit of idol worship and thought it was probably a good thing.

Martin hadn't wanted Merilynn to choose Greenbriar, but it was his own fault that she had. He had fostered her interest in the occult, telling her stories of the Greenbriar Ghost and the legend of Holly Gayle any time she asked. And he had allowed her to go to that cheerleading camp even though he knew full well she had no interest in cheerleading—*Thank you, Lord!*—but was only there to scout for ghosts.

And now, she had entered the sorority that Holly Gayle had been in. Joining Gamma was no different than Merilynn's reason for wanting to go to the cheerleading camp years ago. She simply wanted to live in a house that had ghost stories attached to it. She'd dismissed his generalized warnings about the cult within the sorority as speculation and assured him that he'd done a fine job of raising her, that she could take care of herself.

She had him trapped with that argument and they both knew it. He didn't really know much about the sorority itself—he only held some suspicions based on vague stories. As for the ghosts, well, ghosts couldn't hurt her.

Or could they? He remembered all too clearly the stories she had brought back from Applehead Lake. She'd told him about the island, the eyes, the shrieks, and she'd told him about seeing the ghostly lights of the long dead town, and the apparition that had beckoned to her friend, Sam. They had seen Holly Gayle, seemingly in the flesh.

He believed her stories; Merilynn was blessed with a rich imagination, but fortunately, she knew fantasy from reality and always went to pains to keep the line between them clear, a habit that probably explained why his hair hadn't started to gray yet.

After the camp experience, she took up art, drawing endless pictures of the lake, the ghost, the town, even the eyes. He still had the old drawings; first crayon, then charcoals, a year of pen and ink sketches, and then sheaves of high school—era art. When she turned fourteen, he had given her a set of professional watercolor paints, and that turned out to be her chosen media. By the time she'd gone off to Greenbriar, her work was professional-looking and verged on bursting into a magnificent style. He hoped she wouldn't give up painting, even if what she created disturbed him.

Although she occasionally painted other sorts of pictures, nearly all of them displayed the eerie themes she had fallen in love with at the camp. If she painted a field of wildflowers, there would still be something ghostly about it. It was simply her style and he doubted it would ever change. She loved the supernatural, and there was nothing wrong with that; he loved the study as well.

He had brought her up as honestly as he could, answering questions about life and death, about sex and ghosts and war. The only thing he hadn't been entirely honest with her about was the old chapel in the woods. When she was a child, he had played it down in the stories, and he thanked God or Synchronicity or Chance that she hadn't stumbled on it as a child at camp. Later, when she was in high school, especially when she became interested in attending Greenbriar University, she did some reading of her own and asked him about the old structure. He told her what he knew of it from his books and from stories handed down to him from older folks, but said nothing of his own experiences there, of her tie to the place, and his, and he prayed she would never ask, just as he had always prayed that she wouldn't press him for details about her mother.

Amazingly, she didn't. *Not just amazing, but astonishing.* The girl was born curious, but she asked virtually nothing about her roots. Martin had no living relatives by the time she arrived, but he had had a brother who died young. Fearing for his job if his superiors found out he had a child of his own, he wove a fictional life and marriage for his brother, and then a fictional death.

Later, when Merilynn was old enough to ask questions, he stuck to the story. It was the only thing he could do when she was a child, partly to protect his position but mainly because he couldn't bear to tell her what little he knew about her real mother or about his suspicions about her. Now that Merilynn was grown, when she decided to ask, he would have to tell her the truth. The thought terrified him now almost as much as he'd worried about her mother, in the early years, suddenly showing up and stealing the child back.

The concern faded considerably over the years, rising when she went to the camp so near the chapel, fading more, then rising again when she left for Greenbriar. What if she went to the chapel and encountered . . . something? *Her mother?*

How do you tell your own child that her mother is a demon?

Pio meowed loudly and Martin automatically started to scratch the cat behind his ears, but the animal hissed at his touch and stiffened in his lap. Claws began to dig into his legs.

"Hey, Pio, what's wrong?" He moved his hands away from the cat, who meowed again and then began to purr too loudly and frantically, his body stiff and trembling. Panic seized Martin; Pio had purred like this only twice before, once when he broke his leg as a kitten, and a couple of years later when his hide got caught on the protruding point of a drawer handle shaped like an arrow and frantically tried to get loose before Martin could reach him. There had been little blood, but the six-inch-long gash in his hide had been horribly, obviously painful for many days even though the vet provided pain medication.

During the week that Pio had been barely able to move, Martin changed the drawer handles and Merilynn spent all her free time soothing the feline. That was when she had developed her interest in herbal medicine and in learning to heal with her hands. While he knew the old herbal poultices wouldn't hurt (he had checked with the vet just to make sure) and actually seemed to soothe the cat—since Merilynn added catnip to everything, it wasn't terribly surprising—Martin had never seen any hands-on healing that wasn't of the snake oil variety.

But Merilynn, barely twelve years old, brought home a library book and studied. Within an hour, she was working on the technique, holding her hands just an inch above the wound, her eyes closed, her lips moving silently. And Pio would begin to purr contentedly. When Martin asked what she was doing, Merilynn looked at him as if he were an imbecile, then explained that she was channeling energy from the earth through herself and sending it into Pio to help him get better faster. She invited him to pass his own hand beneath hers when she was working on the cat. Astonishment overcame skepticism when he felt the unnatural heat pouring from her palms. Pio stopped purring and glared at him until he stopped blocking Merilynn's energy. As soon as he moved away, the cat relaxed and purred like a kitten. Martin's hand had felt warm and slightly tingly for an hour after the experience and the vet had proclaimed Pio to have healed faster than he thought possible.

But now, Pio's purr was distressed, not contented. Martin, realizing he was likely to be bitten and clawed if he touched him again, studied his pet, assuming he was in pain.

But Pio's fur had prickled up and he was staring intently at the television screen. Martin looked, saw O'Brien introducing a comic, but nothing else. "Pio?" he murmured.

The cat ignored him. Martin carefully placed one hand on the animal's back, ready to pull away fast, but Pio didn't react. His body trembled with the harsh purrs and nervous energy. "Pio, are you okay?" He put his other hand on the cat's flank and there was still no reaction. Carefully, he began touching the cat, looking for a sign of pain, fully expecting to be shredded when he felt the animal's abdomen, but Pio didn't respond or even move. He was like a statue, a trembling one. And he continued to stare at the screen. Martin did too.

Suddenly he saw something, just a waver in the air in front of the television. It was gone in an instant, but the short hairs on Martin's neck rose on end. "Pio? What do you see?"

As he spoke, he saw it again, the wavering in the air, like heat rising from the black asphalt on a desert highway. If it was possible, Pio became even stiffer under Martin's hands.

The wavering clearness slowly lengthened and began to look like a misty, translucent human form. Martin and Pio watched. As the mist took on a light purplish color, the cat's frantic purring ceased, but he remained tight and stiff. Martin felt fear but also fascination. He watched. He waited.

Seconds slowed and seemed like long minutes as the form grew clearer.

Father!

"Merilynn? Merilynn? Is that you?"

The figure clarified as he spoke, and his daughter stood before him hidden in the rich folds of a velvety deep lavender cloak, except for her coppery hair, longer and fuller than he remembered, falling over her shoulders. Her face looked pale and pure, her Madonna smile exactly as he remembered, and her green eyes . . . They startled him. He had seen them flash with emerald brilliance at times, but now they glowed.

Father!

He saw her lips form the word, but heard her voice inside his head. "Merilynn. What?"

I see you, Father. And Pio. Hi, kitty!

The cat relaxed the instant she said his name. He meowed softly, then stood up and jumped onto the coffee table.

Good kitty, Pio. I miss you.

Pio trilled at her and sat down, his head cocked up to look at her face. *He hears her. He sees her. I'm not losing my mind.*

"Merilynn," he said, "are you all right? Are you . . . " He couldn't say it.

Dead?

He nodded.

I don't think so. I think I'm dreaming, but I'm not sure. Are you real?

"Yes. You are too. You're not dreaming. I see you and so does Pio."

I hope you're right.

"Where are you?"

I'm not sure. It's cold. Very cold. It's dark, too. I had a dream. Maybe I'm still having it. Or maybe it wasn't a dream. I don't know.

"It's okay, honey. We'll figure it out. What did you dream?"

Holly Gayle came to my room. She asked me to help her and the others.

"Others?"

Under the lake. There are so many ghosts trapped there.

"What did she ask you to do?"

I have to find something and then I can set them free. But I'm scared. I can't think. It was clear, but I lost it. I'm *lost. Please help me!*

"I'll find you, Merilynn."

Even as he said the words, her image faded away. Conan O'Brien was saying good night. Pio turned and hopped back into Martin's lap. "I'm sure glad you saw her too."

Pio pushed his head up hard under Martin's chin and purred.

"I love you, too," the priest said as he stood up and set the feline on the couch. Pio instantly curled up in the warm spot Martin had vacated and was sleeping by the time Merilynn's cell phone rang six times and her voice mail came on.

Damn it! Martin went to his writing desk and opened the drawer, stared at the jumble of papers, of bills and receipts. The last time he'd talked to his daughter, she had given him her new roommate's cell number. He'd written it down and put it in the desk. The first thing he had to do was find it.

18

"You passed it," Kendra said as Sam cruised by a mile marker located near the narrow trailhead that led to the chapel ruins an eighth of a mile deeper into the woods.

"We can't park in plain sight." Sam drove on another five hundred feet, then slowed to a crawl and put on her brights. "There's a great place to hide the car right about here."

"You've been here before?"

"I scoped out a parking place when I first came here."

"Why?" Kendra looked at the girl, at the odd expression on her face.

"I intended to check the place out eventually. I like to be prepared."

"What aren't you telling me?"

Sam stared at the road, driving slowly. "I would think you'd be happy I'm prepared. We'd never find a hiding place for the car otherwise."

"I appreciate it, but you seem a little freaked. Why won't you answer my question?"

"There it is." Sam nudged the Camry off the road and eased forward into a grove of pine trees. The space was barely wider than the car itself, but she kept moving forward.

"The ground looks smooth, but the pine needles are really thick. They could be filling a hole." She paused. "You aren't worried about getting stuck?"

"No. I checked it out already, remember?"

Twilight dimmed into near darkness as the car was swallowed by the trees. Sam, looking confident and satisfied once more, cut the engine and pulled the parking brake, then looked at Kendra. "We're her-re," she sang softly and killed the headlights.

"We sure are."

Sam made no move to get out. "Are you sure you want to do this?"

"I'm sure I *don't* want to do this," Kendra said. "But we have to."

"Exactly." With the headlights off, she could still make out the sky, and only ten feet away, bits of the road were visible between the trees. "It's not all that dark."

"Kendra, it's pretty dark and it's going to be totally dark in maybe twenty minutes. But we won't know it because it will seem that way to us in about five minutes, just as soon as we're farther into the forest, away from the road."

"Maybe we should have brought some large men," she joked.

"You're kidding. The large men are all at the football game living up to their IQs. They'd be useless here."

"They're not the brightest bulbs, but they'd be

nice to have along in case we run into the local serial killer."

"Okay, that's true. And if we run into any ghosts, it would be fun to watch them run off, screaming." Sam stared at her. "If you want to do this, let's do this."

Kendra nodded. "How do you feel about it?"

"I feel like I'm the idiot girl in a horror movie who walks up the stairs by herself. My feeling is that this is too stupid of an idea to even consider. But I also feel like we need to do it."

She released the trunk latch, opened her door, and stepped out, went to the rear of the car. Kendra did the same. By the little courtesy light in the trunk they opened their backpacks and removed the books they'd piled in to hide their flashlights and light-sticks.

"What else have you got in there?" Sam asked.

"Water, some Band-Aids, and aspirin. And pepper spray." She took the small canister out and clipped it to a belt loop on her jeans. "And this," she said, showing Sam her sharp silver letter opener. "It's sort of an heirloom and it could pass for a knife."

"No, no. Don't put it back in your bag. Put it where you can get at it quickly."

Kendra's heart raced as she carefully slipped it into the long pocket inside her denim jacket.

"I've got this." Sam showed her a metal rod, less than an inch in diameter and only about six inches long.

"That's a weapon?"

"Uh-huh."

"Is it a martial arts thing?"

"No. It's a billy club."

"Don't you think it's a little short?"

Sam smiled and hefted the metal rod, pointing it away from Kendra. She flipped her wrist and Kendra heard a disturbing metallic sound and saw the rod shoot out a full eighteen inches. "Okay, I believe you. That's a billy club."

Sam tapped it, releasing the springs, and the rod slipped back down and became an unimpressive six inches again. "I like it," she said. "I wish I'd thought of pepper spray too, though." She put the rod in her pants pocket, shut the trunk, and said, "Let's go."

"Wait." Kendra searched for the right words, then decided to be as blunt as Sam. "You never answered my question."

"Which was what?"

"Have you been to the chapel before?"

Sam didn't answer for a long moment. Finally, she said, "Yes. When I was at camp."

"You and Merilynn went there?"

"No. Just me."

"Something happened."

Sam nodded. "I don't remember much about it and it's not pertinent to why we're going now. I'll tell you some day."

"All right." Kendra swallowed and squared her shoulders. "I'm ready. Let's go find Merilynn."

19

Father and Pio faded away like phantoms as Merilynn began to notice the smell of old, damp wood. Next, she recognized the cold scent of the lake and the sound of water lapping and sloshing below her and the unmistakable muted knock-knocking of small boats moored and gently sloshing against the dock.

Am I awake? Or am I dreaming?

She opened her eyes but the view didn't change; there was only darkness. Wanting, needing to know if she was awake or dreaming, even if she was alive or dead, Merilynn searched for clues by calling upon her other senses. She lay on her back on an uncomfortably hard, ridgy surface and realized it had to be the old damp wood she was smelling. Her body, which she hadn't even been aware of until now, felt chilled to the bone, stiff and achy. She welcomed the pain.

I'm alive and I'm awake!

She decided to sit up and did so without mental effort—further proof she was truly awake at last. Rubbing her hands together so fast and hard it ought to have started a fire brought only a bare hint of tingly warmth, but it was enough for the time being.

Her mind was beginning to function better as well. Endless dreams of being lost, wandering in Applehead Forest, trying to contact her friends and, last, Father for help, still muddied her mind. It had seemed so real. She still felt lost and she had no idea where she was.

That's not true. You're sitting on a dock at the lake. You're inside a boathouse.

There were several little docks with boathouses scattered around the lake, so what she didn't know was which one she might be in. Or how she'd gotten there, but the cobwebs were clearing. It would come back to her. It had to.

Cautiously, she got on her knees, then felt around to determine the width of the dock. *At least five feet.* Satisfied, she started to rise, then lowered herself back down as she realized she had no sense of direction. It was safe to bet the planks ran across the width of the dock . . . Wasn't that how all docks and piers were built? Suddenly, she wasn't so sure. But even if she was right, standing up to walk would be foolish; she might walk straight off the end of the pier, right into the lake.

And judging by the damp feeling of the Levis she wore, she'd already taken a dip. With a sigh, she put her hands flat on the wood and began to crawl, hoping she'd chosen the right direction.

20

The forest was quiet but not silent, and for that little bit of normalcy, Sam was grateful. A light wind stirred the leaves of the oaks studded among the pines, and their sounds reminded her of sheets flapping on a faraway clothesline. Every so often, a stronger gust caused a flurry of golden leaves to let go of their branches and sprinkle down on them in gentle waves.

Night birds called. Now and then some small creature would scuttle through the underbrush, making sounds too small to cause alarm. Kendra's flashlight lit the narrow worn path, and while the trees loomed tall and close, Sam felt none of the claustrophobic heaviness that she had felt long ago and expected now.

"Any idea how much farther we have to go?" Kendra asked in library tones.

"I've never been on this path before but it's supposed to be only a little over an eighth of a mile to the ruins from the road. It can't be much farther."

They walked another ten feet before Kendra remarked, "This isn't so bad." "I'm not getting goose bumps, or anything. I thought I'd be terrified. Instead, I'm just a little nervous."

"I know what you mean. When I was in here as a kid, the atmosphere was different. Heavy. Nasty-feeling. You know what I think?"

"What?"

"I think the weather must have a lot to do with how people perceive this place."

"You mean like when the barometer rises or falls?"

"That's exactly what I mean. Tonight, the air is dry and the wind feels light. Does that make sense?"

"Yes," Kendra said. "The wind feels playful. More kid-Halloween-spooky fun than seriously scary."

"It does." Sam squinted into the darkness ahead and thought it seemed less dark. "Hey, raise your light a little—I think the clearing is ahead."

Kendra lifted the lantern higher and pointed the beam ahead. The beam wasn't terribly strong, but it was enough to show that the trees lining the path gave way, letting some dusky twilight in another hundred feet or so. Something skittered through the bushes to their right and Kendra swung the flashlight around, looking for the source of the sound. And found it.

"What's a chipmunk doing out at night?" Sam asked. The cute little creature sat up on its haunches, sniffing the air and staring at them.

"For all I know, they come out at night. Don't they?"

The chipmunk chattered, then raised its striped tail and scampered down the path, disappearing in seconds. "Maybe there are nocturnal types."

Kendra shrugged. "Shall we?"

They began walking to the end of the path and a moment later, came to the clearing. They paused there, still sheltered by the trees, and silently studied the black outline of the ruins, still vaguely visible despite imminent nightfall. Sam looked up at the sky. The waning moon was up; that had to be helping.

After several silent moments, Kendra said, "I don't think anyone's here."

"Neither do I." Sam stepped into the clearing, gesturing to Kendra to follow.

Turning on the lantern, Kendra joined her, playing the light around the boundaries of the round meadow, then over the ruins. Nothing moved. She illuminated the broad empty doorway, saw only grass inside. Then she put the light back down, angled over the ground. There was slight evidence of a path, but it was overgrown with grasses. She glanced at Sam, who nodded.

Keeping the lamp pointed just ahead of them, Kendra and Sam crossed the meadow and stood in the doorway of the chapel. Kendra used the light to check the interior for dangers. "Safe," she said softly.

They entered, walked to the end, where grass gave way to dirt and ashy wood remnants in a thick circle of smooth, smoke-blackened stones. A faint odor of burnt wood hung around the firepit. Sam squatted, examining the bonfire leavings more closely. Her nose twitched at the strong scent. "This was used recently."

"Today?"

Touching the stones, then a chunk of wood, mostly burned, she said, "No. At least not for a couple of hours. I'd guess this is leftovers from last night, or even two nights ago. I don't know enough to be sure." She rose and they walked around in the small building. Above, the slice of moon was bright enough to make her squint, and when she looked away, she saw its afterimage.

"This is interesting," Kendra said, taking a few steps toward a large vague rectangle where the grass was sparser and shorter.

Sam stepped onto the area. "It's softer. But if it was a grave or something, it's been here long enough for the grass to start growing again. I'm sure Merilynn's not down there."

"It's peculiar though."

"Definitely. But it's not what we're looking for."

Kendra cast the light around. "The grass looks trampled."

"Sure. There were people here having a bonfire."

The girls in dark hooded cloaks. They stood around someone who was tied to the ground. One of the cult members had a knife.

"Oh, my God," she said softly. Her voice trembled, her heart pounded as details cleared.

"What's wrong?"

"I saw someone killed here when I was a kid."

"The serial killer? You saw him kill someone."

Sam shook her head. "I wish. No, it was a coven. I heard singing and followed it from the camp. I thought it was beautiful. Then I stood right outside that window"—she pointed—"and saw them. There was a fire roaring. They were in a circle around a naked girl. Then their robes came off and they were nude underneath. They stood back—that's when I saw the girl tied down on the ground. The priestess

had Cleopatra makeup on. She had a black knife."
Sam paused, trembling.

"Are you okay?" Kendra murmured.

Sam sucked it up. "I'm fine. The victim saw me.
Her eyes—she was terrified. Then the high priestess
kneeled over her, raised the knife, and plunged it in.
The sounds were horrible. I think the cult was singing,
but I'm not sure. Then the priestess pulled the girl's
heart out of her chest and held it up." Sam hesitated.
"And she saw me."

Angry chittering made them both jump. Sam
swung the light around. The little chipmunk sat, not
five feet away, staring at them, cursing in Squirrel.

"Let's get out of here," Sam said.

"Let's."

They moved rapidly toward the exit.

21

The chipmunk watched them go, then raced around the interior of the chapel, examining everything. It had already done so before the girls arrived, and been satisfied that nothing damning was obvious. The grass, helped with a touch of magick to grow rapidly carly that morning, after Jenny and Ginny were done burying the bodies, was not yet as long as the surrounding growth—even her spells couldn't do that, not without the help of the Puckwudgies, who were disinclined to cooperate with her. In the dark, the lack of length was barely noticeable, yet the Gamma freshmen *had* noticed.

Disconcerted, the elemental decided it didn't matter—Brittany and Malory would return together in a few hours to cast a spell that would instantly disintegrate the bodies, making them indistinguishable from the soil unless someone knew to take samples for microscopic examination. But no one would, and the grass would be look no different from the older greens by morning; the short patch would be gone.

Everything was fine, except, perhaps, for one little thing.

When Samantha Penrose had said she remembered seeing a sacrifice here years ago, the little elemental had been shocked. Although Malory and Brittany hadn't attended Greenbriar University as sorority sisters that year, they had come for the sacrifice, as they always did. The Greenbriar Wood—it had only become Applehead Forest in the nineteenth century—was the elemental's natural home and so the Forest Knight of Greenbriar had become Malory's personal patron when she took Brittany as her familiar. (That was how Malory saw it, but the truth was that Brittany had chosen Malory.)

The elemental's rapid-fire thoughts returned to the words of Samantha Penrose. Malory had worn ornate makeup, as she always did for the summer sacrifices, so there was little chance Samantha would know it was her.

And only Malory had seen her; Brittany herself had stood opposite her, her back to the window, and had barely sensed something amiss before Malory, full of power instantly after the sacrifice, wiped the little girl's memory clean. The Fata Morganas hurried out of the chapel before the knight's arrival, and Brittany never even thought of the incident again until, later, Malory spoke of it.

The little girl had grown and now lived in the sorority house among them. Worried, the chipmunk took off, racing through the woods, back to her mistress.

22

"You said what happened to you at the chapel when you were a kid at camp wasn't pertinent to our trip tonight," Kendra said after Sam backed the Camry out of the grove and pulled onto Applehead Road. "Where are we going?"

"The road's too narrow here; we'll have to go a ways before we can turn around." Sam turned her brights on, illuminating trees that seemed to lean forward, looming over the car, edging the curving road, old and evil. "As for pertinence, I said that because I honestly couldn't remember what I'd seen. All I knew was that the place frightened me and I thought there was probably a reason."

"So, the sacrifice . . ."

"Remembered it while we were standing there." She laughed nervously. "I'll tell you, I about wet myself. Suddenly, I could see that girl spread out on the ground, and that face that looked like Cleopatra, you know, in that ancient Liz Taylor movie?"

"I remember."

"Only this priestess or whatever she was, she wore

even more makeup. Her face was white—too white. It was makeup, I think, not a mask. I remember noticing that the whiteness blended away into normal pale skin at the base of her neck."

"Her hair?"

"Black, Cleo-style. I think. I was fixed on her eyes. They were all edged in black. I swear, when she looked at me, my mind just filled up with those eyes, and then—nothing."

"What happened after that?"

"I don't know. I wandered in the woods and finally found my way back to the camp." She paused. "I've always known that part though. I think I got lost. I sneaked into my cabin not very long before dawn."

"So you have some missing time."

"Maybe, maybe not. It was really late when I went out."

"But the priestess saw you. She didn't just let you go, did she?"

"Kendra, if she didn't, would I be here? That has to be how I got lost—running away in a blind panic."

"We've seen things, Sam. Like what Merilynn did. Maybe she made you forget."

"Oh, please. Spell-casting? I doubt it. I know what Merilynn can do and I don't deny what I've seen, but there was nothing supernatural going on in that chapel. Just some sick satanic cult getting their jollies. I was a kid. I repressed the memory." She slowed for a hairpin curve, laughed once, a bitter sound. "After that, I was decidedly uninterested in going into the woods. Merilynn and Eve were going to walk this little nature trail that loops up behind the camp the next day and I made up some excuse so I wouldn't have to go with them. The truth is, I was terrified."

"Are you still?"

"Hey, I walked to the chapel in the dark with you, didn't I?" She slowed as they approached a wide spot in the road, nosed into it to make a U-turn. She pulled forward, letting the engine idle, the high beams lighting the road and the other side of the woods. "I don't really like Applehead Forest, though," she admitted. "I don't really like any forests. Maybe that will change now that I remember what happened."

"Well, I've got to hand it to you, Sam. I couldn't have gone into that forest tonight if I felt like that to begin with. You're the bravest woman I've ever met."

"No, I'm not. I never would have done it on my own."

"Sure you would."

"No, not alone. I only managed to walk in there because I had you there to watch my heroic act." She looked Kendra in the eye, embarrassment showing. "By myself, quivering jelly. I'm just a show-off."

Kendra smiled and patted her knee. "Hey, whatever works. Some day, when I write a book about the history and legends of Applehead Forest, you'll go down as the warrior maiden who dared enter the chapel at night despite the horror she'd seen there as a child."

Sam snorted. "And who will you go down as?"

"The narrator." She grinned and said archly, "I shall be your humble Boswell."

Sam laughed, all traces of anxiety vanishing. "You're full of it. I'm no warrior maiden."

"Hey, it works for me."

"Okay, but change my name. And don't tell the story for at least twenty years, when those cultists are too old to track me down."

"Deal."

23

Merilynn's hand touched empty air and she knew she had crawled the wrong way along the dock. Exhausted, she lay down flat on her stomach, hand still extended over the water below, turned her face to one side, and pillowed her cheek with her other hand. Almost too tired to shiver, but not quite, she rested and remembered.

The room at Gamma came back to her; she recalled how they'd seen the ghosts of Holly and Eve on the lawn below, and that Malory and Brittany had encountered them. She remembered sitting on the floor playing the Ouija board unsuccessfully with Kendra, trying to call the ghosts. And then they had gone to bed—and the phantoms came into the room, just as she was drifting off.

They spoke to Kendra, but mainly to her. *How much did Kendra hear?*

If she hadn't run off so quickly, if she'd compared notes with her roommate, at least, then she'd know if help might be on the way. Her impression was that Kendra had heard little before falling asleep. *They made her fall asleep. I think.* Why hadn't she at least left a note that would help Kendra locate her? *That was really, really stupid, Merilynn!*

Sleepy and cold, hunger a gnawing ache in her middle, she thought through what she had heard, her heart skipping a beat as Holly Gayle's words came back to her. *The living daughter of Malory Thomas can release us.*

Merilynn's mind had reeled. If she hadn't been lying down, she might have fainted. She dared not believe what had popped into her mind, not until Holly answered her question:

You know I am speaking about you. You. The sorceress appeared to your father and used his seed to conceive you. Your father is the priest.

Does Father know he's my real father? Merilynn had asked.

Yes. He knows many things. He can help you.

On some level, she knew it was true. She had always suspected that Uncle Martin was her true father, but had sensed from earliest childhood that it was not a question she should ask; instead, she called him Father. And she had never dared ask about her mother, not because Martin gave off a don't-ask vibe, but because she knew it was better not to know. Instead, she embraced Delores, her nanny, Martin's housekeeper, as her mother and pushed her questions down into a deep, dark place inside herself.

Deep and dark, like her mother.

But how can I be Malory Thomas's daughter? She's not old enough to have a daughter my age.

It made no sense, but it was true. She remembered Holly's words: *the sorceress and her familiar. They are dangerous.*

Her mother was a sorceress. She might be any age. She might be an old crone who cast a spell to appear young and beautiful. She might be able to shape-shift. And Brittany . . . *a familiar?* Merilynn had never thought of familiars as more than companion animals. When she was younger, she'd called Pio her familiar. Father had laughed and told her not to say that in front of clergy or parishioners. It had never been more than that, but now, she realized, there could be. *What is Brittany?*

She's an elemental. Puckwudgies were elementals, but not the same kind as a familiar would be. They were fairy folk; familiars were animal elementals. Different. *But how?* Her drowsy mind clawed for answers. Familiars would be stronger, she thought, more dangerous to humans because they could be seen by anyone, if they wanted. *What is Brittany?* she wondered again. *A raven? A wolf? A cat? Something else?* She thought of the girl's bright eyes and her penchant for nuts and sunflower seeds. An image emerged in her inner eye. *An elephant.*

If she hadn't been so tired, she would have smiled. In truth, she was probably a bird or maybe a squirrel. *Or a monkey.*

I have to get out of here. She used that thought to attempt to chase away the nonsense, but her mind refused to cooperate, returning instead to Holly, and how she had revealed the silver athame with the glowing green stone in its haft. She had told her, *You can release us and all those others trapped under the lake if you can find this dagger and kill your mother. It is the only way she can be killed.*

Where is it? Merilynn had asked.

I will show you in your dreams.

The apparitions disappeared and Merilynn tried to talk to Kendra, wanting to know what she had heard, but she couldn't get any words out, couldn't even make her muscles obey her orders to sit up. Sleep took her.

And, later, just before dawn, the dream had come.

24

"She *what?*" Malory demanded.

Brittany sat on a stool behind the big claw-foot tub and rubbed her mistress's bare shoulders. "She remembered seeing the sacrifice," she repeated. "But that's all. She told Kondra that it had to be a satanic coven. Relax, your shoulders are like steel."

"Exactly what did she say?"

Brittany told her what she'd heard in the knight's chapel, massaging as she spoke. "There's no need to worry. She specifically said she saw no magick."

"And why did she say that?" Malory twisted her neck to look at her familiar.

"Kendra suggested her memory had been removed by a spell."

"She *what?*" Malory demanded again.

"Relax. Give me the soap. Thanks." She lathered her hands in the oatmeal-coconut foam from the bar, then slicked the fragrant bubbles over Malory's neck and back. "You know Kendra's into the folklore stuff. And she's experienced your daughter. It's no surprise. Do you think she hasn't figured out that

Merilynn caused the 'food poisoning' and the periods? Hell, she was probably there, with her. But I doubt that Samantha was, because she laughed off the suggestion of a spell to erase her memory. She said she'd simply blocked a horrible memory and shamed Kendra for thinking otherwise."

"Is Kendra going to be a problem, do you think?"

"Perhaps. You know," she added, squeezing water over Malory's back, washing away the soap, "she might make a decent sacrifice."

"No." Malory spoke flatly, without hesitation. "Why not?"

"I've known her family for generations. So have you, remember?"

"Oh. She's the one descended from all those housekeepers. They lived in Applehead before it was drowned."

"Right. And then in Greenbriar. They're coastal now, but Kendra's grandmother is still alive. She worked here for a short time. She saw Holly once. And I'm sure Kendra's mother knows the stories. And Kendra. With her interest in folklore, it's not surprising she's here, although I heard her admit her family isn't pleased. Harming her or letting her find out too much would bring us too many problems."

"Why did you decide to let her in then?"

"For fun. Or maybe tradition. Her ancestors were canny women, worthy of respect. She is as well, unless I'm very much mistaken. We won't be at this campus after this year, and she might make an excellent leader for the Gammas."

"But not the Fata Morganas."

"Of course not. You realize she suspects we exist."

"Does she?"

"Of course." Malory's shoulder muscles finally began to loosen. "She has to suspect because of her family history. The whole mystery surrounding Gamma intrigues her. But she's safe."

"What makes her safe?"

"She's content with legends and folklore. She's far more interested in stories than in truth. In fact, I'm sure she would rather have the mystery than the facts, so in her own way she will protect Gamma, even though she's not a Fata."

"Maybe she should become one of the inner circle then."

"No. Brittany, surely you can sense her true spirit."

"She'd never go along with the sacrifices."

"Never. Brush my hair, please. I can imagine Merilynn or Samantha coming to our side if we had devised the right methods of manipulation." She shook her head. "I had such high hopes for Merilynn. She's full of power and she's attracted to her roots. Ah, well."

"What about Samantha?"

"She is ruled by her need for knowledge and power. We'd just have to shut off her interest in telling secrets to bring her in. In her own way, she would make a superb Fata Morgana. Alas, I doubt we can turn her."

"Why not?"

"She has an annoying streak of morality that I fear we can't undo. It's too bad we didn't procure her years ago, in one of our high school programs. Then we have the fact that she's the girl who saw our rites, happened to join *our* sorority, and has overcome the spell of forgetfulness I cast. *No one* can resist that spell. But she did. Subconsciously, she has probably never entirely forgotten; that's what brought her to us." She smiled. "It's too bad we can't use her tenacity."

"She's our sacrifice, then," Brittany said. "Oops." The brush clattered to the tile floor. She picked it up and continued brushing. "You have such beautiful hair. It's like silk."

Malory made a purring sound in her throat, but a column of bubbles from her rear accompanied it, bursting to the surface like little blossoms of nuclear waste. The mild sexual excitement that had begun building in Brittany's loins was abruptly fumigated.

"Sorry," her mistress said.

"Your problem is no better?"

"I think it's less frequent now."

"But no less fragrant." The brush slipped out of her hand, hitting the floor. "Oops, I did it again." She bent and picked it up.

"You're clumsy tonight."

Brittany didn't answer, but concentrated on relaxing her mistress before she told her the rest. Finally, when Malory started making little sounds of contentment, she told her, "I was so worried about getting back and telling you that Samantha is the girl who saw us performing the chapel rites that I didn't tell you the rest."

"Mmmm. Well, it could be no worse than what you've already said. What is it?"

"Remember the reason you asked me to follow them in the first place?"

"Of course." Malory sat up, stiffening again. "Of course I remember." She sounded defensive, which meant she had forgotten. She only forgot things when a sacrifice was missed and the Forest Knight's gift of continuing immortality became overdue.

Malory could go far longer than this without making a blood sacrifice before any real deterioration showed, but the others, the purely human members of the sisterhood of Fata Morgana, would exhibit symptoms much sooner. Their smaller powers would wane quickly, skin would loosen, hairs turn grayer and grayer until the sacrifice was made. It was really rather fun, as far as Brittany was concerned. Especially when certain girls—*Heather Horner*—who had become a little too full of themselves experienced a taste of mortality.

"What did you learn?"

"As you thought, mistress, they were looking for Merilynn. They said very little, but they obviously didn't know where she is. I'd guess they were simply looking in a place they thought was logical."

"Dry me." Malory pulled the plug on the tub and rose, her body dripping. She held her arms out as Brittany wrapped a thick sage-green bath towel around her. Malory tucked it over between her breasts and stepped out of the tub. "The chapel is a logical place," she said as Brittany took a smaller towel and began drying her arms. "If Holly asked for Merilynn's help to find my stone. Where did they go from there?"

Brittany laughed. "Back the way they had come. Something frightened them."

"The knight?" Malory asked sharply.

"No, I didn't sense the knight. I believe it was simply Samantha's memory of the sacrifice that stampeded them."

Malory smiled. "Stampeded?"

"Yes." Brittany moved to her mistress's legs, not bothering to tell her that she had scared them herself. Malory would be displeased by that.

"It took much bravery for them to even enter the chapel," Malory said. "The wards we set around it scare off all but the most determined humans."

"Or the most insensitive." As she spoke, Brittany worked her way up under the towel, dabbing away water droplets from Malory's inner thighs, praying to the Forest Knight that her mistress wouldn't emit any gases as she worked to distract her from her worries. "Tell me, mistress. What are your plans for this evening?"

"I've decided to give Professor Tongue the night off, due to this problem." She punctuated the comment with a nasty little poot.

Brittany leaned back on her knees too fast and tumbled onto her back. Malory laughed. "I just wanted to see if you were paying attention, little one."

"Very funny."

Malory let the bath towel drop from her body. "Finish me off, will you?"

"I'll finish *drying* you if you promise no more surprises. I *won't* finish you off. Not until this noxiousness passes." Brittany, back on her knees, resumed drying the sorceress.

"Come on, Britt," Malory said, pushing the blonde's head crotchward. "I need more than drying. The good professor has earned a reprieve. But you are my servant." She pushed harder. "Give your mistress a little kiss."

Brittany rarely minded playing the subservient

role; that's how it worked between a sorcerer and a familiar. But she would brook no humiliation. "No. Let go."

Malory laughed, low and throaty. "Do as you're told."

Brittany, hiding her fury, bent her head to her mistress's private triangle and gently bit a lip.

"That's it." Malory pushed her head closer, urging her to get to work.

Brittany, still holding Malory's sensitive flesh between her teeth, willed herself to change form. Suddenly, there was a faint stirring in the air; then Malory shrieked.

"Let go of me, you little bitch!"

The chipmunk sank its teeth in as Malory tried to pull it away.

"Ouch! Stop it!"

Brittany didn't stop, even though she could taste that she had broken the skin.

She heard the door slam open and a feminine voice shriek, "Oh, my God, Malory, you've got a chipmunk on your pussy!"

"Don't you think I know that?" Malory screeched, yanking the rodent off.

The elemental recognized the voice as not belonging to any of the officers—the only Fatas senior enough to know what she really was—and let go of Malory as the other sister approached. Malory loosened her hold and the chipmunk dropped to the floor, then scurried across the room and out the open window.

Hiding just out of sight, she chittered madly when the other Fata, Helen Bach, an infant of eighty-some years who still looked eighteen, cried, "I've heard of perverts putting gerbils up their asses, but what on earth were you trying to do to that poor little squirrel?"

25

"You can come out now," Malory said. "Helen's gone. The door is locked."

Her familiar hopped onto the open windowsill, chattering madly.

"I won't try to force myself on you again. I promise."

The chipmunk swore eloquently, wanting more than a promise.

Finally, Malory caved. "I apologize, okay? I'm sorry. You're my familiar. You always do things like that for me. You're supposed to take care of me."

The chipmunk crossed its tiny arms and glared at her.

"I apologize. I love you. What more can I say?"

The creature hopped into the room and the air wavered. Brittany stood before her mistress, arms still crossed. "You know what you have to say."

"I'm your mistress. I don't have to say anything, except that I'm sorry if I somehow offended you."

Brittany let her true nature burn through her blue human eyes, turning them dark as night and as sparkling as diamonds. "How soon you forget that this is all a convenient game. A tradition among your kind and mine." She stepped forward and Malory backpedaled. "Have you forgotten, *mistress,* the true nature of our relationship?"

Malory didn't reply, but looked at her defiantly. Brittany could sense a silent glamour being hastily woven.

"That won't work. Remember the last time that your pride forced me to remind you of the truth? You tried to cast a spell on me then, as well. You cannot."

"I can."

"Not without the Forest Knight's gift. And even then, it won't hold." Brittany pinned her like an insect under glass. "Don't forget which of us is his favorite."

Defiant, chin tilted up, Malory glared at Brittany.

"We have work to do, sorceress. Admit your place and it shall be done. Refuse, and suffer the consequences. The knight is already displeased with you."

"And you," Malory said softly.

"No. I am pure. I am part of his world. You are half human. Your mistakes are not mine. I *help* you perform magicks and glamours. I *help* you with the sacrificial rites that keep your beauty and immortality intact. I need no such rites. I am forever."

"A familiar is a minor elemental, nothing without a mistress or master."

"Not so, *mistress.* You merely wish to believe that, and while it's true that my kind benefits from a relationship like this, yours benefits much more."

"You are bound to me."

"Of my own will. Familiars are loyal folk or I would have deserted you long ago. You're not the only maker of magick in this land, you know." Brittany let her elemental soul continue to shine through her eyes to hold Malory in place, but now she smiled as well. "I am fond of you, Malory. I was fond of you from the moment we met, when you were still Morgana, only a few centuries old, a mere babe barely out of her mentor's arms, so quickly into mine.

"Remember how I helped you attain the favor of the Forest Knight so that you no longer had to travel back to the old world to appease a much harsher Green Master? You told me all about him. What he did to you, to your body, ripping you apart with his lust, then rewarding you as you lay dying, with healing and renewed beauty? Do you want to go back to that cruel master? If I tell the Forest Knight you've fallen from my favor, he will not look kindly on you anymore. He already watches you closely. You have lost the precious gift he gave you, so now you must make many more sacrifices to atone. You failed to deliver your most recent sacrifice, a very important one, as you know, and judging by his actions last night, I dare say he's very angry and *very* hungry." She paused for effect. "I don't think you should anger me, either, *little one*." She spat the words, advancing on Malory, backing her into the wall. "What say you?"

"I say—"

Brittany grabbed her roughly by the shoulders and lifted her from the ground as if she weighed nothing. It was a move she knew Malory despised.

"I say that you are dear to me."

Brittany let her drop, adding a mental push that threw Malory to her knees. "What else have you to say?"

"You are, in truth, my mistress and I am your loyal servant." She bowed her head, cheeks flushed with humiliation and, most assuredly, her own fury.

Brittany had to fight to keep from giggling her delight as power shot through her, her own and Malory's, and satisfaction, too. Years of frustration melted away, just as they always did when it was necessary to put her sorceress in her place.

Sexual energy filled Brittany. She began to undress, knowing the power the mere sight of her human body had over true humans, wanting to do to Malory what she had tried to force her to do. Looking down at her humbled mistress, Brittany decided that Malory could do with a bit more discipline, so she indulged herself. Continuing to undress, she dropped her Gamma T-shirt on the floor, unzipped her jeans, and stepped out of them. Finally, she stripped off her red thong, the one she had stolen from the drawer of a new sister a month ago.

Naked and perfect, oozing sexuality from every pore, she put her fingers beneath Malory's chin and made her look up. The sorceress trembled, not with fear, but excitement. She craned her neck forward, licking her lips in anticipation, salivating at the sight of the elemental in human form—no human could resist such a thing, not when there was no clothing to dull the auric emanations.

"No," Brittany told her firmly. She laid her hand against Malory's forehead and pushed her away.

"Why not?" Malory's whisper was strangled with desire. "Let me apologize. I know you want me to."

"You've already apologized. Now you shall pay penance by looking at what you cannot have. Now, it is time for us to work." She turned and crossed the suite, intending to sit down at a small round table covered with green silk, then noticed Malory hadn't moved, but stood, statuelike, drinking in her body. "Come here! You're no goggle-eyed human. You should not be so entranced that you can't move!"

Malory approached, her gaze unwavering.

Brittany pointed at her own face, as she let her eyes blend back down from diamond-black to their usual shades of blue. "Eyes up here, sorceress."

Slowly, Malory managed to meet her gaze. There was such desire and longing evident in her face that Brittany, who did love the magickal old bitch after all, took pity and pulled a green cloak from a wall hook and drew it around herself. She sat down. "Get the black mirror and bring it here. Sit down and we shall scry until we find your wayward daughter."

26

Sam gripped the steering wheel tightly to keep her hands from trembling as she and Kendra approached the turnoff for Greenbriar University. Although she had admitted that she'd been frightened, Kendra couldn't possibly know just how bad the scare had been, and Sam wasn't about to tell her. Pride, plus a very real fear that admission would make what courage she did possess blow away like a dandelion puff on the wind, kept her quiet.

"We're almost back," Kendra said.

"Yeah, we are."

"The game probably isn't over yet. If we go back to the house, it'll be pretty empty."

"Malory will be there. And Brittany. They didn't look like they were going anywhere."

"True. That's a good reason not to go back yet." A car turned onto Applehead Road from the Greenbriar turnoff up ahead. Sam dimmed the high beams. "It's early. Do you want to do something? Get something to eat? Pizza?" She paused. "Maybe we should stop at the house and see if Merilynn's back."

"She's not."

"How do you know?"

"I have my cell." Kendra patted her jacket's breast pocket. "Merilynn left hers in our room and she already put my number in her phone's memory. She'd call."

"I'm convinced. We won't stop," Sam said. "So, shall I cut through the campus toward town or stay on Applehead and go around it?"

"Bypass," Kendra decided. "I hate crawling through all those stop signs and drunken frat boys."

"I agree."

They passed the college turnoff and continued along the long loop of road. The forest narrowed quickly on the campus side, disappearing completely when the road turned east. To their right, the forest looked impenetrable; on the left, the stadium came into view, brilliantly lit and full of people. Even with the windows up, Sam could hear the muffled roar of the crowd. Something in the sound chilled her.

27

The sorceress and her familiar sat bent over the round oak-framed mirror that covered a good portion of their small table. Together, they murmured words of a language spoken only by those with intimate knowledge of the ancient ways of the otherworld, a place few humans experienced for more than a fleeting instant during their little lives. If they experienced it at all.

Their differences forgotten, their palms lay flat on the green silk cloth, fingers touching, their bodies exchanging energy, the two building more together than either could hope to alone. The symbiotic bond, forged throughout centuries upon centuries, served them quickly and well now, despite Malory's still feeling slightly weakened.

Minutes after they began reciting the words of power, the shiny black surface of the scrying mirror appeared to waver and shift, rivulets of black on black shimmered with metallic ores within its depths, sifting like desert sands. Before long, the mirror took on form and depth that even a simple human might have been able to see.

"Show us where Merilynn is. Show us my daughter," Malory said in the strange lilting tongue. Brittany asked the same.

And waves appeared on the mirror's surface, small and whitecapped. A mound appeared in the center of the mirror, ugly, not unlike a monstrous head rising from the black water. Applehead Island.

Malory studied the water, looking for the gleam of ghost lights beneath the lake, but saw none, at least at this distance.

The edges of the lake became clearer as more power words were spoken and although the aerial view was of the night, details became fairly easy for Malory's eyes to discern and even easier for Brittany's. There, on the northern shore, were little squares and rectangles; that was the boys' summer sports camp.

On the southern shore lay the cheerleading camp, looking much like the boys' camp. It had smaller cabins, and more of them, and the dock jutting from the boathouse at the lake's edge was slightly longer than the one at the other camp or either of the smaller ones dotting the eastern and western shores not far from the boys' camp.

At one edge, the clearing bearing the knight's chapel was partially visible, the outlines of the ruins stark black and white shadows. They could discern the faintest green glow coming from within and around the roofless building; it told them their wards were intact, ready to frighten off trespassers. It was the color of magick, the color of the Forest Knight.

The roads and school were not visible. Brittany

and Malory exchanged glances. Merilynn Morris was somewhere within this view. "Closer," Malory commanded. "Show me the island."

The mirror shimmered, dissolving and resolving in the space of fifteen seconds. Now only the island was in view. They examined it, looking for signs of Merilynn, for signs of magick. The only thing there eminated from the black pit on the island's center, a bare green mist that phosphoresced from the frequent presence of the Forest Knight, who often dwelt within the caverns below.

Strange words poured from Malory's mouth. They commanded a closer look at the cheerleading camp. Again, everything shifted and shimmered as the psychic telescope adjusted itself. The flagpole, flagless, appeared. The white spotlight was off. Below it, a few tall sodium lamps glowed among the trees.

"Closer," Brittany murmured.

Again, the vision shifted. They seemed to hover just above the buildings now. Electricity sparked between the pair's fingers as they moved, as one mind, around the buildings, seeing nothing, but sensing something. Without speaking, they examined the edges of the buildings, swooping down for a new view, looking into black windows that were fiercely and suddenly unshuttered by the force of their will.

"She's not there," Malory said.

"The boathouse," Brittany murmured. "We haven't looked there yet!"

The view now was one that they would have if they were watching the feed from someone walking through the camp with a minicam rolling. They approached the lake's edge. The visible dock was boatless and lonely, and the boathouse, built on a double-wide platform that was part foundation and part dock, looked deserted.

There was a single door on the dock that led inside, plus wide garage-size doors at either end. The building had no windows.

Malory examined the edges of the doors, thought she saw a faint glow from within. She glanced at Brittany, who nodded; she saw it as well.

"She's in there," the familiar said.

"We have to be sure. Quietly, the door on the dock."

"It's locked. If we rip it, she'll know we've found her."

"She had to get in there. The big doors are padlocked."

As Brittany spoke, their view returned to the single door. A padlock gleamed in a hasp there as well. "I still say she's in there," she told Malory.

"Inside a building locked from the outside."

"This one, yes."

"She swam under the door."

"Of course."

"Shall we?"

"No." Malory disliked the water; it was the home of Holly Gayle, and the prison of many, many more. While she did not fear the dead, she preferred not to encounter them. She pointed at the old-fashioned rusty doorknob with a large skeleton keyhole. "Look through here. Close now!"

"Damn it!" Blackness filled her vision. "It's blocked."

"I can see that," Brittany said in the soothing voice that Malory hated because it meant she expected her to lose her temper or act impulsively.

"Don't speak to me that way!"

Brittany ignored her outburst. "We have to go under the water to see in." She paused. "Would you like me to look?"

"Don't be ridiculous," Malory said sharply. "We aren't actually there. I'm not afraid of getting wet."

"What are you afraid of?" the elemental asked in the same soothing voice.

"Nothing, you little bitch!" Red filled her vision, staining the blackness of the mirror's view of the boathouse.

"Calm down!"

"Fuck you! Sometimes I think you provoke me on purpose!"

The vision shimmered. Brittany looked impish and innocent.

Malory cursed, drawing the image back to the mirror, clarifying it before it could escape. Ignoring Brittany, she moved to view the the wide double doors on the shore end of the little boathouse. She drew a great surge of energy from Brittany and from within herself, and the doors burst open. Looking past the boats, Malory saw what she wanted at the very end of the boathouse's platform.

"There she is! Let's go get her!"

The image swirled and disappeared, leaving the mirror's surface shining smooth and black.

Brittany stood up and shed the robe. Malory averted her eyes; now was not the time to let desire overcome her.

"How do you want to get there?" Brittany asked. "Are you strong enough to open an aport?"

"Yes."

Brittany leaned over and began tying her shoelaces

as Malory got up and found a black sweater and jeans, dressing as quickly as she could.

"I thought you wanted to follow her," Brittany said as she pulled a black hooded jacket over her own dark shirt. "What happened to your plan to have her lead us to the gem?"

"We'll still do that."

"You weren't subtle, Mal. She probably sensed us when you destroyed the door."

Malory slipped on laceless black running shoes. "You think so?" she asked, dripping sarcasm. "I'm altering our plans. With Samantha and Kendra searching for her, we can't just let her run free. We'll bind her and force her to talk."

"Bind her?" Brittany's eyes gleamed, darkness coming into them. "In the caverns?"

"Where else?"

Brittany grinned approval. Grabbing a handful of peanut M&Ms from a bowl on her dresser, she walked up to Malory and held out her hands. "Ready to transport?"

"No. Let's go outside. The less matter we have to travel through, the happier I'll be."

"How's your stomach?"

"It's getting better, I think. The cramps are less intense."

"I noticed you haven't been perfuming the air quite so much."

"That means we'd better hurry. If Merilynn's spell is weakening, she may be dying. We can't let that happen again."

"Again?"

"We need her to find the stone. And perhaps as a

sacrifice. I think she would please the Forest Knight, don't you?"

Brittany smiled and popped candied nuts into her mouth, then held the door open and locked it behind them. "Where do you want to transport?"

"The back lawn."

"Someone might see."

"Behind the smokehouse then. Let's just get the hell out of here!"

28

Merilynn was having the dream again. She knew it was a dream, knew she was resting on a boathouse dock in reality, and flying with Holly and Eve on the astral plane.

Not flying. Swimming. In the lake.

Holly smiled at her. *Do you remember what you did after I showed you this last night?*

Yes.

That was how she'd gotten wet. She had gone to the boathouse at the old cheer camp and was looking for a way to break a lock so that she could steal a boat that would take her out to the site of the old town of Applehead. There, she intended to dive—she was an excellent swimmer—and retrieve the stone in its daggerlike casing. It hadn't gone quite as she expected.

It was daylight when she arrived, and the camp was locked up tight. She was searching for something, anything, to use to break into the boathouse, when she heard the rumble of an approaching vehicle. She moved to the far end of the boathouse and stood in the shadows, hoping she wouldn't be spotted by whoever was coming.

A dark green custodial pickup truck came into view. Merilynn clung to the edge of the shadows, desperate not to be seen as the driver pulled up to park right next to the dock. She took one too many steps backward and, with a splash, fell into the water.

Crap! Afraid the custodian would investigate the splash, she did the only thing she could think of: she dived down and swam into the boathouse.

Freezing cold, she had waited for the men—she could hear them talking to each other, shooting the shit about cranky wives and ungrateful children. What they were doing there for so long, she didn't know. What little she'd seen appeared immaculate.

But they wouldn't leave. Eventually, she recognized the sound of aluminum lawn chairs opening, the slide of a tray being set up, even the hiss of beer bottles being opened. The men were having a leisurely morning of man-gossip and beer and, finally, lunch. It was endless.

Hey, Joe, look what Carla packed for me. Pepperoni and onions on a torpedo roll. All thin sliced, must be half an inch of meat on there. And just the right amount of mustard. And look, I got a big kosher dill! No wonder I put up with her shit. She knows how to feed her man.

As foul as the sandwich normally would have sounded, Merilynn's empty stomach yearned for it.

Nice out for this time of year, huh, Earl? Sunny and warm. Though I sure wouldn't want to go swimming. My nuts'd shrivel up into little raisins and drop right off and Shirley wouldn't be real pleased about that. Man, that woman can go down like the Titanic *when she wants something.*

That's how come she's always got those nice new clothes?

Yuck, yuck, yucks all around. Yeah, that's how she gets her clothes. Keeps me broke, but who the fuck gives a rat's ass? The woman's a Hoover.

Carla's always bitching about Shirley's clothes.

So feed her a meat sandwich and buy her some. I got kids to put through college.

Fuck that. Let 'em earn scholarships. Hey, I got cards. You wanna play some poker?

Shivering cold, exhausted, starving, and just generally miserable, Merilynn waited for them to leave. The thought of using a spell to get rid of them hadn't even occurred to her. *Idiot!*

Now, gliding down through the water, guided by ghosts, Merilynn realized she hadn't thought of it because she was meant to wait here. For this moment.

I wish I remembered the dream.

Holly sent a good feeling to her, a sort of warmth. *Dreams fade. Your first plan was too hasty to work. If you had tried it, you might have drowned. Do you remember where you were going? Where the gemstone in the sword is?*

In the town.

Yes.

Amber lights began winking on below them. Delighted, Merilynn watched the picture she had painted so many times come closer and closer. She felt as if she were gliding among the stars.

It is beautiful, isn't it?

The message had come from Eve. Merilynn smiled at her.

The gemstone is very powerful, a gift to your mother from the Forest Knight. I took it when she killed me, greatly diminishing her power. But she is very dangerous even without it. She wants it back. It is safe from her here, hidden in plain sight, but we are trapped here with it.

Merilynn watched the lights grow, but turned her thoughts to Holly. *What do you want me to do? Hide it somewhere else so you don't have to guard it anymore?*

Holy smiled sadly. *If only it were that easy. We are trapped here with or without the stone in the sword. That's what it is, a miniature broadsword, not a dagger or any other blade. We are trapped here until Malory Thomas is destroyed. No one but blood can do that.*

Suddenly, very close, the stained glass steeple in the old church burst to life. Merilynn stared at the beauty of it, a beacon in the watery night. The colors, ruby, emerald, sapphire, and sunlight, were clear and perfect. She strained to make out the design.

Only you can destroy her and you need the stone and the sword to do that. The blade holding it is strong, full of magic. The stone and the sword are objects, without allegiance, and you will be able to turn the blade against her. You must kill her.

Where is it? Merilynn gazed, awestruck, at the beauty of the stained glass. It was a picture of the forest and Applehead, the tiny town in a green valley full of orchards, green leaves, red apples. It was a picture of the past.

Here! Look here and you will see it!

* * *

An explosion of wood as the double doors came off their hinges yanked Merilynn back to her sleeping body. She sat up, saw the pale sand that seemed to glow in the dark, saw the flagpole, some camp buildings dabbed with sodium lights. The doors were gone, only a few shards remained, a jagged black frame for the beach beyond.

Water sloshed, boats jostled for space, the building creaked. Merilynn shivered, still damp after a day in this dank place, and started to rise, then felt her back pelted with lake water. She turned, and peering at her, her head just above the dock, was Holly Gayle, white with death and cold, all the friendliness and warmth hidden in her haunted eyes.

Run! She knows you're here. Run!

29

"Have you ever tried Thai Gonzales?" Kendra asked as Sam slowed the car to a meek twenty-five miles an hour as they entered the quaint little speed trap named Greenbriar.

"I haven't," Sam admitted. "I thought about it, but I don't have much spare cash, so I hate to take a chance on wasting it on food I'll end up throwing away." She smiled. "Or throwing up. So, have you tried it?"

"No, but Eve did." Kendra hesitated, when the dead girl's name popped out of her mouth, then pushed on. "She said it wasn't half bad. She advised against getting any dishes that were Thai-Mexican mutations though."

"Smart girl." Now Sam felt the discomfort. "I wonder which half isn't bad."

"I'm guessing the half that isn't mutant food."

"Do you want to try it?"

"Do you?" Kendra countered.

"I love satay. Did she say anything about that?"

"Not that I recall. It's so hard to find a place with

good peanut sauce for satay. Most sauces suck. But I'll probably try it anyway. When it's good, it's to die for."

Sam snorted. "Too bad Brittany isn't here. I'll bet she could give us a rundown on the quality of the peanut sauce. I've never seen anyone down so many nuts."

"She's always eating. But it's not just nuts. She loves chocolate too."

"So she's normal?" Sam grinned, feeling the best she had all day.

"I wouldn't call her normal. She should be a lard-ass, the way she eats. Oh, turn right here."

Sam turned. "She goes for all those early morning runs. That must be her secret." She paused. "You know, I've watched her. She doesn't run around the campus like the rest of the joggers."

"No? Where's she go? There's the restaurant." Kendra pointed at the modest THAI GONZALES sign glowing like a big postage stamp above the door of a building a little ways down the street.

"Evidently, she runs in the woods."

"Really?"

"Yeah." Sam pulled past the restaurant, skipping perfect curbside parking in favor of the last slot on the block.

"Why down here?"

"In case we want to make a fast getaway. Remember last night?"

"God, that seems like weeks ago. You never stop thinking, do you?"

"I try not to."

They got out and locked the car, both stuffing

wallets into their pockets instead of carrying bags. "Hey," Kendra said. "Wait a second. Unlock, please?"

Sam did. Kendra opened the door and moved her long, sharp letter opener from the seat to the floor, pushing it out of sight, under the seat.

"You sure you don't want to carry that?" Sam smiled, but she meant it.

"No, I'll stab myself." She patted a pocket. "I've got my pepper spray, though. What about you? Are you packing heat?"

Sam snorted again, knowing it was two too many times for one evening, but feeling comfortable enough to give in to the old kid-habit. "I've got my little friend Roddy right here."

"Good. If we run into those wrestlers without Merilynn along to do her tricks . . ." Her expression changed instantly.

Sam locked the car again and stepped onto the sidewalk, touched Kendra's shoulder. "Hey, don't worry. Merilynn can take care of herself. She's fine."

"Yeah. I'll keep thinking good thoughts."

"Really, Kendra," Sam said. "It's going to be okay."

"How do you know?"

"I just feel it."

"Reporter's instincts?"

"No, just my feeling. Come on."

They walked a short half block to Thai Gonzales and looked in the big glass-front windows.

"This place looks suspiciously like a dive," Sam said.

It was bigger and brighter than Greenbriar Pizza, a simple place, the walls lined with red leatherette booths, the center cluttered with tables and chairs that looked like refugees from a 1970s kitchen. The tables had avocado-green metal legs, as did the dinette chairs. The chairs seats and backs had been recovered with the same red leatherette material as the booths, and red and green lights were strung along the ceiling, giving the place a distinct run-down trailer-park Christmas aura.

Ceiling fans turned slowly and a bored-looking girl stood behind a cash register, staring at them without seeming to see them.

Still the place was half full. "It couldn't be too bad, with this much business," Sam said.

Kendra was perusing the menu in one corner of the window. "It's affordable. I think we're safe as long as we don't order anything with mystery meat ground up in it."

Sam opened the glass door. "After you, madam."

30

The moment Malory and Brittany hugged themselves together in the shadows of the smokehouse
and began reciting the spell to open the aport to take
them to the Applehead Cheerleading Camp, Brittany
could tell her sorceress was still handicapped by
Merilynn's spells and, probably, her own overindul-
gence the night before. Generally speaking, crea-
tures who belonged in the sorcerer category had
iron constitutions, but now and then one could be
thrown out of kilter by the tiniest things. It all had to
do with gravity and weather and body chemistry,
along with at least a dozen other boring subjects. It
simply happened, and that was that, end of story as
far as Brittany was concerned. Whatever spell Merilynn had cast would be stopped the moment they
bound her.

The aport wasn't opening. "Mal, concentrate,"
she said, not admitting she had let her own mind
wander off. "I can't do this all by myself."

"I'm trying."

"You're very trying." Brittany gave her a soft,

moist kiss to boost her energy and her spirits. "Now, again."

They repeated the words, and this time the aport opened, surrounding them, carrying them toward the camp. She hoped. Aports and deports were peculiar anomalies. In the last few decades, she had been amused by the science fiction shows that unknowingly dealt with them, calling them wormholes and who could remember what else? And then there was *Star Trek.* For a time—several times, actually, as the series' popularity would peak yet again, evidently blessed with more lives than a cat—senior Fatas, even Malory herself, the queen of all Fata Morganas everywhere, had taken to calling transporting or teleporting "beaming." Brittany hated it so much that she had beseeched her lord, the knight, to stop her mistress from using the term. Offering up a trio of greasy disco boys she'd picked up at a club in Caledonia, she begged for help. The knight, pleased with her offering, stripped the white polyester suits from the young men, then stripped them of their skin, spitting out the fake gold chains and medallions.

The knight liked skin. Brittany thought of it as his version of an appetizer. After he had flayed the disco boys, he granted her wish, giving her the power to cast a spell of her choosing to stop her mistress. And ever since, whenever anyone said, "Beam me up, Scotty," Malory was afflicted with burning nipples. Not literal burning, of course, Brittany had no desire to harm her sorceress, but the sensation of fire, white-hot heat, engulfing them. It happened so rarely that Malory had never caught on, and even if she had, what good would it have done? She wouldn't have suspected her little Brittany, not in a thousand years. Or even two thousand. Once, right after the spell was cast, Malory said the fateful words herself in a restaurant in Seattle. Instantly, her expression had changed from pleasure to horror and she'd grabbed her glass of iced tea and Brittany's glass of iced water and sunk her tits in them, sighing with relief, ignoring the staring customers. The spell only lasted for thirty seconds at a time, and when the half minute had passed, she had Brittany help her cast a glamour over the patrons to make them forget what they'd seen. And to humiliate them a bit as well.

But it was a nice kind of humiliation. Malory did love that group orgasm spell of hers. She did it often enough that she packed a wallop all by herself. When Brittany joined in, if there were more than a dozen people present, it was a sure bet that at least one would suffer a heart attack.

Reality wavered around her within the realm of the aport. It wasn't like *Star Trek*, not at all like *The Time Machine*. Instead, it was a place outside of time, where even she had no sense of time passing. It was eternity and a billionth of a trillionth of the blink of an eye at the same time. How you experienced it pretty much depended on your mood.

Now, it seemed endless. Brittany put her effort back into concentrating on the trip. This was a place like the eye of a hurricane, where nothing was stable, and to move out of the eye of the storm at the wrong time could be disastrous, even deadly. Especially for part humans like Malory. They could get lost if they traveled without their familiars to guide them, and even with a familiar along, many a sorcerer had lost a limb when he or she wasn't cautious enough about keeping appendages tight against the body. They never knew it until they reached the deport, either. One familiar, a crow named Shalkinaw, a nice enough elemental despite its penchant for fireworks at inopportune moments, had a master, an old white-beard like Malory's had been, who tilted his head back to yawn and lost the entire top of his head. When they reached the deport, Shalkinaw said that the old wizard looked puzzled, reached up to scratch his pate, and stirred what was left of his brain into mush.

We mustn't let that happen to Malory, even if she deserves it. Brittany tightened her hold, again forcing herself to concentrate. Familiars who took on animal forms always suffered the effects of the animal's true nature. Brittany had a yen for nuts and seeds, and for sex, and a tendency to pack away bags and cans of nuts in her home, a trait that grew as the weather turned cold. Her biggest problem, however, was keeping her mind on one thing for very long. It moved rapidly, taking in everything, remembering the important things, forgetting the rest. Transporting was difficult for her when it felt like eternity instead of fractions of instants.

Concentrate!

Out of time and space, she planted her lips on Malory's, bringing both of their minds into focus.

Instantly, they arrived at their destination, or close to it, she thought. Trees surrounded them.

"Where are we?" Malory asked, sounding out of breath. Transporting was hard work.

Brittany scanned, finally spotting a cabin. "We're here. The camp. Come with me." She took Malory's hand and led her toward the cabin. There, the rest of the camp was revealed, and it really was the right camp. Beyond the cabins, the lake glistened darkly. "Are your eyes adjusted?" Brittany asked. "Can you see well enough to run?"

"Yes."

"Let's go, then."

They raced out of the woods and down to the boathouse. She was slightly surprised to see that the doors really had been blown off their hinges. That rarely happened.

"Look what we did," Malory murmured, pride in her voice.

"A little showy, don't you think?" Brittany asked, thinking of her old friend, the grandstanding Shalkinaw.

"Definitely not subtle. But I think—yes. See her aura? She's still in there. We've got her!"

31

No sooner had Holly Gayle told her to run than Merilynn had turned to do so—but silhouetted in the gaping doorway were two figures, one tall, one short. Both bitches.

"Why, if it isn't Mommy dearest and her little dog, Toto," Merilynn said, knowing she was already dead. None of her piddley spells could get her past these two.

Malory stepped toward her, Brittany at her side. "Come here, Merilynn. We've been looking for you all day. Kendra and Samantha told us they were worried."

"You lie quite well," Merilynn said agreeably. Her eyes darted, seeking escape.

"They're looking for you, too. They'll be so relieved that we've found you."

Brittany spoke those words and they sounded truthful. Merilynn paused, taken in for just a moment. She wanted to believe them, wanted to be taken home and dressed in warm clothes, placed in

front of a fire, and fed hot chicken noodle soup. *No,
they'll feed me to the fire!*

"You're an even better liar, Toto," Merilynn told
Toto.

"Don't call me that, you little—"

"Hush, Brittany," Malory said, snakey-soothey.
"This is my daughter, my only child. My heir. Merilynn, please come to your mother."

Something icy cold touched Merilynn's ankle.
She barely refrained from jumping, then managed to
look down with only her eyes. A white hand had
emerged from the water. Fingers tapped her ankle.

Dive into the water, Holly Gayle said. *It's the only
way out.*

"Merilynn," Malory said, moving slowly forward,
"please come to me."

Something in her voice mesmerized Merilynn.
Something in her eyes drew her.

Look away! Holly cried in her head. *Look away!
She's hypnotizing you.*

"Merilynn, darling. All these years separated from
you, I've been miserable. And I was afraid to tell you
who I really am." Malory's voice broke, right on cue.
"I was afraid you would reject me. But now you
know. Please, please love me as I love you."

"You don't know the meaning of the word!"
Merilynn turned and leaped into the lake.

Holly and Eve were waiting. They pulled her down,
away from the surface, away from the shore.

Deeper and deeper they went, and Merilynn began
to struggle against them. *I need to breathe! Let go! I
need air.*

Trust Holly, Eve murmured.

Merilynn's lungs burned as she looked into Eve's ghostly face. *I'm dying! Please, let me go!*

You'll truly die up there. Holly stared into her eyes, her face a bare inch away. *She will take your soul.*

Merilynn saw lights twinkling to life in the depths before them. *Applehead!*

Yes. Holly's face seemed to engulf hers. Then everything winked out.

32

"Crap," Kendra said, a forkful of fragrant jasmine rice poised before her lips.

"The food's not all that bad," Sam replied, swirling a thin piece of chicken in peanut sauce. "And at least it's bright enough in here to see the cockroaches before they can walk onto your plate."

"I'm not talking about the food," Kendra said dryly

"What are you talking about?"

"Look up."

Sam raised her eyes. "Crap," she agreed. "How'd you know they were coming in? Do you have eyes in the back of your head?"

"There's one of those giant spot mirrors mounted near the ceiling behind you."

"I knew that." She made a face to show she *should* have known that. "Cheerleaders. They're traveling in a pack. Not a single jock among them. That's odd."

"Do you think so? Eve said they do a lot of group

bonding, even more than the sorority sisters do."
Kendra sipped her Pepsi.

"On a Friday night?" Sam asked. "That's a date
night, isn't it?"

"I don't know. I haven't had a date since I've been
here."

"I haven't either. What about that guy I've seen you
talking to. Jimmy? Johnny? He's in my public speaking
class. And he's in at least one of McCobb's classes."

"I'm not sure . . ."

"He has dreadlocks. Sensitive type but he shows
up plain as day on my straight-dar."

"Jimmy, sure." Kendra grinned. "He's pretty cute,
isn't he?"

Sam chewed. "I've seen worse."

"He's smart, too."

"In that case, I've seen *a lot* worse."

"He asked if I wanted to do a study date with him
for McCobb's class."

"And you said?"

"Yes. But I don't know when it'll happen.
Everything's so messed up." Kendra raised her voice
as the din of cheerleaders started to drown her out.

"Listen to them," Sam said. "No wonder there
aren't any guys with them."

Kendra and Sam had chosen a small booth at the
rear of the restaurant, looking for peace and quiet.
The music playing on the loudspeakers wasn't too
soft or too loud, but just right to cover the low mur-
murs of conversation in the place. Until now.

"They're coming our way," Sam said.

"I can hear them."

"And see them. Are they nice and distorted, all
round in the middle?"

Kendra chuckled and checked the mirror. "They are. Lord, listen to them. I'm embarrassed to be female. They really do sound like clucking hens. Do you suppose we sound like that too?"

"We? You mean us studious types?"

"Sure. I meant nerds, but studious types sounds better."

"We can't sound like that. Our voices don't go that high and our lips don't flap that fast. Shit, they sound like they're all doing speed."

"It's that purple juice they swill. You know about that? Eve said Frau Blucher passes it out to them before games. It's a real pick-me-up."

"Frau Blucher? That sounds familiar."

"Cloris Leachman in *Young Frankenstein*. The horses went nuts any time her name was spoken."

"An apt name for Mildred McArthur, then." Sam picked through her rice, looking for things that didn't belong in it. "I've seen them drinking that juice," she said. "It's always in the refrigerator."

Kendra nodded. "In the jug labeled 'cheerleaders only.'"

"I might take a sample and get it analyzed sometime."

"Why doesn't that surprise me?" Kendra's good mood grew a little despite the clucking girls in green and gold. "Listen to them. Can you tell what they're saying?"

"I guess I could if I zoned in on one conversation. All I get is pissed off and bitchy in general."

"We must have lost the game." She paused. "Wait. I know what it is."

"What?"

"Merilynn's spell. They're all on the rag."

Sam laughed. "Let's hope we get out of here alive, then."

"Hi, girls. Where's Merilynn tonight?"

Heather Horner planted herself by their table, her tanned midriff at Kendra's eye level. A couple of the J-clones flanked her.

"She's around," Sam said, looking her straight in the eye. "Do you feel okay, Heather?"

"Of course I do. Why?"

"You look, I don't know, unwell."

"What do you mean?"

"A little puffy." She smiled sweetly. "That time of the month?"

Kendra couldn't help it. She giggled.

Heather glared daggers at her. "What's so funny?"

"Oh, I'm sorry. It has nothing to do with you. Sam told me a joke just before you came up and I just got it."

"Tell it to us," Heather said. The clones agreed.

"You wouldn't like it," Sam said, shooting Kendra a confused look.

"Sam's right, you wouldn't like it."

"Why not? You think it's funny." The three cheerleaders moved closer, bullies in short skirts and sports bras.

"Well, since you insist." Kendra smiled low and slow. "Do you want to tell them, Sam, or shall I?"

"You go right ahead. You're good at telling jokes."

"Okay. Well, there's a woman, and she walks into a drugstore to buy tampons. She sees a display of tampon boxes stacked on the end of an aisle with a sign on them that says 'Five boxes for a dollar.'

"Well, she just can't believe the price is that low, so she asks the clerk if it's correct.

"He says, 'Oh, yes, five boxes for a dollar.'

"She replies, 'That can't be right!'

"The clerk says, 'Lady, the sign's right. Five boxes for a dollar, no strings attached.'"

Sam shook with laughter and Kendra burst with it. The cheerleaders simply glared at them.

33

"She's dead," Brittany said, scanning the lake. "She's never come up and she's not hiding under the pier."

"She can't be dead. I need her." Malory's lower lip stuck out.

"Mistress, no one can hold their breath this long. I spent half an hour alone watching under the pier while you watched the water. If she was there, I would have seen her come up for air."

"Damn it. Damn it. Damn it. Brittany, maybe she already has the gem. If she does, with her bloodlines, she might be able to do just about anything I can do."

"But you've been doing what you do for centuries. She's new. She wouldn't know how to work the stone."

Malory crossed her arms. "She's drowned. But she's a swimmer. I remember that from her application. She was asked to be on her high school swim team repeatedly. How could she drown?"

"Holly took her," Brittany explained. Seeing the

look of understanding bloom on Malory's face, she added, "Holly, two. Malory, zero."

"Shut up." Malory paced ten feet of shoreline, paced back, did it again. "That dead bitch is going to pay. I'm going to squeeze her until I get her soul; then I'm going to put it in the bottom of a pit toilet on Pike's Peak. We'll just see how she likes that."

"Grow up, Malory. Think about it. She's building her army. She's got two souls, plus a few more and all the half-wit ghosts down there. This is war."

Malory paced some more. "It sure is. Where's my cell phone?"

"I'm not your secretary. I didn't bring it." Brittany dipped into her pocket and produced peanut M&Ms, crunched them up. "I'm your chipmunk. I brought what I like." She stuck her tongue out, covered with chocolate that was busy melting in her hands.

Malory stalked up to her and embraced her. "Let's go."

"Go where?"

"Back to the house. To my suite. I need to do the voice-shifting trick and make a couple of phone calls so no one will worry about Merilynn. Now, put your arms around me and start chanting."

34

Merilynn left her body when its heart stopped. Suddenly, she was free, swimming along with Eve, trailing Holly, who had somehow morphed around Merilynn's head and upper body, engulfing it in her own.

What's happening? Where are we going? Frantically, Merilynn looked around with eyes that could see far more clearly underwater than ever before. The lights of Applehead were behind them. Ahead, lay only darkness.

We're going to the island, Eve told her. *Holly's taking you there. It's safe.*

Excuse me if I'm wrong, but if I'm dead, isn't everything pretty much safe?

Eve reached out to her, twined her phantom fingers in hers. She felt real. She felt alive, not icy cold. *Hurry! We have to keep up.*

Merilynn surged forward without effort. Holly?

She can't answer you. Not right now. Eve squeezed her hand. *You're amazing. So powerful. Holly couldn't have done this before.*

Confused, Merilynn asked, *Done what? What are you talking about?*

Your body. She's using your power to save it. You don't think a spirit could move a body on her own like that? She can save you because of who you are. And with your help . . .

I know. I can set you free. The island loomed. Holly swam down and around the earth, leading them into a watery cavern, then straight up. Merilynn surfaced, treading water, blowing water from her mouth, taking deep breaths. Only she wasn't doing any of those things. It just felt as if she were.

We have to help her now. Eve half swam and half glided toward Holly, who had unwound, returning to her normal form. She held Merilynn's head above the water just below a smooth scoop of rock.

Help me lift her.

It was a peculiar sensation, trying to lift her own body. Merilynn's hands kept going through the physical form. Eve had only slightly better luck.

Holly smiled softly. *We have the power to do this. All you need is intent. Know, beyond all doubt, that you can lift this body. You can. Once it's out of the water, it will be in the knight's care.*

Merilynn and Eve tried again. Eve succeeded quickly, and soon Merilynn got the hang of it. They pushed her body—*so white, so thin*—onto the ledge, then moved back. Holly began to sing an old song, "Greensleeves," in a high pure voice.

Why? Merilynn wondered.

She's calling the Forest Knight. He usually comes to her when she sings this melody. It's beautiful, isn't it?

It was. Merilynn listened, waiting, watching, wanting to ask so many questions, knowing she couldn't, not now.

And then she felt him. The Forest Knight, lord of this land, one of her fathers. His presence filled the chamber before she even saw the green glow of his eyes.

When she did see them, she knew them. This was the bottom of the cave she had leaned over to peer into so long ago. The eyes had met hers. She was frightened then, but not now. Now, she was awestruck. The eyes neared, a dark form becoming visible as it descended to the ledge.

Heal her, sir, Holly asked. *This is your daughter, of your own blood. She wields great power. We need her.*

Merilynn made out a suggestion of a leafy face behind the eyes. They traveled from Holly to Eve and finally came to rest on Merilynn, on her spirit. He held out a hand.

She swam to him.

He embraced her spirit and, overcome, she clung to him. Her body lay dead at her feet but she had never felt so full of life, so wonderful and rich. She dared not look at him, not yet, but pressed against him, melding with him.

Drink of me, daughter. I am your strength.

Merilynn looked up and saw the eyes, not human, nor inhuman, not cruel but firm and full of love. He had leafy vines for hair and beard and when he smiled his green smile, she relaxed against him, content.

Merilynn.

Holly's voice brought her back to the world—whatever this world was—and she saw the two phantoms waving. *Don't forget us,* Eve called.

We shall see you again.

Holly's words faded like an old echo and the spirits disappeared beneath the black water.

The Green Man cradled her spirit in one hand and scooped up her physical body in the other. Then he began to climb, humming some strange but lovely lullaby.

Rest, daughter.

35

Heather and her clones continued to loom over Sam and Kendra. Sam was about to say something rude, but Kendra's phone shrilled in her pocket.

She pulled it out and punched it on. "Hello?"

Sam watched her face; first seeing open mouthed surprise, then a slow smile that turned into a grin capable of lighting up the whole room. Kendra had a finger pressed in her free ear to block noise, so Sam turned her attention to Heather. "Did you want something?"

Heather shrugged, her eyes on Kendra's animated face.

"Hell, yes, you had us scared half to death!" She looked up at Sam and mouthed *Merilynn*. "You're sure you're okay? When will you be back? Uh-huh."

Sam gestured at the phone and said, "Let me talk to her."

"Just a sec. Sam wants to ball you out for running off without telling us. *Yes,* you deserve it." She laughed. "Here's Sam."

Sam grabbed the phone. "Merilynn?"

"In the flesh." It was Merilynn's voice, all right, with her distinctive lilt that made her sound happy even when she wasn't.

"What happened to you?"

"I was just doing my thing, you know, trying to find Holly Gayle. I told Kendra the details."

"Details? You were on the phone for two minutes, three tops."

"I just went out to the lake and looked around. Then I decided I was getting way too into this stuff, you know, obsessive, and I decided to take off for a while."

"Where are you?"

"Up north, staying with an old friend, right near Big Sur."

"What's your number there?"

"I'm calling from the general store. Rebecca doesn't have a phone in her cabin. Isn't it quaint? She's elderly. You know how *they* can be."

"Quaint is one way of putting it. So how do we get in touch with you?"

"I'll have to get in touch with you." She paused. "I have to get some downtime, you know, away from the school. It's been getting to me, all the ghost stuff."

"I thought you loved that stuff."

"Well, I do, but I mean, *really,* I hiked to the lake in the dark, by myself. Even I know that's a dumb thing to do. Rebecca is a witch. A wiccan, you know, a white witch. She's going to tutor me in herbs and potions and I'm going to stay away for a while. I need a rest."

"What about your classes?"

"No biggie. I'll drop out for a while, then drop back in. Maybe."

"Maybe?" Sam asked. "What do you mean, maybe?"

"I might not come back. You know, the whole place is just sort of creepy."

"Did something happen to you?" Sam asked sharply, instincts up.

"No, why?"

Sam paused. "No reason. Is your uncle coming for your things?"

"No. I told him it was just for a couple weeks. He understood." She cleared her throat and Sam thought, for just an instant, she heard giggles in the background. "Honestly, I probably *will* be back in a week or two. Or three."

She heard laughter again. "Is that Rebecca laughing?"

"Uh-huh."

"I didn't know witches were silly. They seem serious."

"I'm a witch of a sort, and you *know* I'm silly, Sammy."

Sammy? Merilynn never called her that; no one did, and lived. Ignoring it, she said, "I hope you enjoy your vacation. Is there anything you want me to tell Jimmy?" She drew the name from the air, thinking of the boy with dreadlocks.

"Jimmy?" the voice lilted.

"Come on, Merilynn. You told us all about him already, so don't be coy."

She laughed a little too quickly. "I know I told you about him, Sammy, and thank you, but I'll call him myself. If you see him, tell him I'll be inviting him up to the redwoods for some sexual magic."

"Will do," Sam said. "Listen, Merilynn. Keep in touch."

"I will. 'Bye."

Giggles speckled the background until the connection cut out. Sam handed the phone back to Kendra, who kept up her smile for the looming cheerleaders.

Sam looked up and gave Heather a Mona Lisa smile. "That was Merilynn."

"Oh?"

"She's said to tell everyone hello. And then to tell you good-bye for a few weeks while she takes a little trip."

A skeptical look from Heather. "In the middle of the term?"

"You know Merilynn," Sam said breezily. "She's a free spirit. Hey, I see some jocks coming in. Maybe you'd better go cheer them up."

Heather turned and stepped away, the Js following, then she threw Sam a dirty look when she saw a decided lack of jocks.

"Just keep going," Sam urged, barely loud enough for Kendra to hear.

The cheerleaders kept going, over to a table of their own kind.

"So?" Kendra asked, sitting forward. "What was all that about?"

"Whoever it was, it wasn't Merilynn."

"Are you sure? It sure sounded like her."

"Yeah, well, *this* Merilynn says she's going to call Jimmy and invite him up north for some enchanted loving."

"Who's Jimmy?"

"I made him up. A test. She failed."

"So what do we do?"

"We stay very quiet. I think we're up against some nasty people."

"Malory and Brittany?"

Sam nodded. "And probably the rest of the secret sisterhood. The voice imitation was absolutely uncanny."

"What put you on to her?"

"Giggling in the background. Somehow an old lady who practices witchcraft and lives like a hermit in a forest doesn't seem like a giggly type to me."

"What do we do now?"

"We act normal and we go back to your room and go through her notes and things. We need to find out what's coming up, occultwise."

"Halloween," Kendra said promptly.

"That would be a big night for sacrifices."

"The biggest."

"Anything before that?"

"Not unless it's something special to the society. I'd say Halloween's a safe bet."

36

"They bought it," Malory told Brittany, purring like a contented lioness. "Merilynn's priest father bought it and her brilliant friends bought it."

"They couldn't help buying it. You shift voices like a true elemental."

Malory beamed. "Do you think so?"

"I do." Brittany flopped back on the bod and held out her arms.

Malory slid into them. "There's so much to do. We need a sacrifice. We need to initiate our new Fata Morganas. We need—"

"Each other," Brittany interrupted. "We need each other for now. Mistress, you performed so well tonight. I'm sorry you had to lose your daughter, though."

"I lost my sacrifice." Malory nuzzled Brittany's neck, kissing and nibbling. "She was only good as a sacrifice. But what a grand one she would have been."

Brittany stroked her hair, lost in thought. Malory was wrong to assume the Forest Knight would want his own daughter for a sacrifice. Malory was rarely wrong, and never so wrong as this. It was disturbing. Very disturbing.

"Britt?" murmured the sorceress.

"What, love?"

"Make love to me."

"I shall."

"Now."

"Patience, mistress." She rolled away and rose, her eyes on Malory, questioning her motives, her reasoning. It made no sense. Or perhaps it just appeared that way. "I'll be in the shower for five minutes. Be undressed when I return," she said, blowing her a kiss.

Even Malory couldn't tell that her smile was false.

All Hallow's Eve

37

The final two weeks of October passed in a flurry of fiery colors as orange, red, and yellow leaves dropped from the liquid amber trees on the Greenbriar campus. The forest turned from green with dabs of gold to a mix as the oaks were finally overrun by their aging gold coin leaves that chattered on the chill breeze.

Pumpkins sprouted on porches. Professor Tongue had three on his and replaced them each time they were smashed by drunken frat boys. By night, he gave tongue lashings to the president of Gamma Eta Pi. She wore him out and often brought along luscious little Brittany to double his pleasure. Tongue knew that he would never be honest with Malory about his preference for her bubbly blond sidekick, because if he told her she would never bring her to him again. Malory was a breathtaking bitch and somehow, when she was around, he could refuse her nothing. He was happily whipped. Relatively happily, at least.

The days passed and pumpkins appeared and

reappeared on his porch and two insatiable females did the same in his bed. All was right with the world. *Almost.*

Almost because Malory had him too whipped. She was more than an insatiable bed partner; she had become a problem in his public speaking class. She disrupted everything with her bizarre—granted, very entertaining, but still bizarre—talks, and he didn't know what to do about it.

He couldn't take her to task like a normal student; as often as not, he wore her scent to class, just a subliminal suggestion, the rest washed from his upper lip with water but no soap, so as not to totally destroy the memory. He couldn't help it; he was that smitten.

And in private? He didn't even dare to bring up the subject of her disruptive speeches. He dreaded her anger though he'd never seen it, and as Halloween drew near he realized that he was afraid of her, of what she might do to him or to his class.

That turned him on. And since he could never quite remember how the classes ended, it couldn't be all bad. He kept telling himself that.

The Monday before Halloween, Malory had soared to new heights with a speech she called, "You Are What You Eat." After announcing the title, she proceeded to give an excellent and fascinating talk on the ways men could improve the taste of their bodies, their sperm in particular. No one's attention wandered as she waxed eloquent on avoiding dairy, caffeine, and smoking "if you want your honey to be more willing to provide oral pleasure."

When he made his weak protest about content, as he always did, she merely smiled and explained that even some presidents of the United States didn't consider this act to be sex, so hers certainly couldn't be considered an obscene speech. She then went right back to her speech, adding that even worse for fragrance and flavor than dairy products, which putrified and befouled the "natural masculine nectar," was the lowly asparagus stalk. No one, she said forcefully, cared to taste semen laced with that particular thistle.

She had lightened her tone then and suggested that women should feed their men sweet fruits to give them a "pleasant sugary flavor."

Tongue didn't remember much about the speech after that, but she deserved an A. No one held the class's interest like she did. Quite possibly, no one even dared to try.

And so, Halloween arrived for Professor Tongue. Alone in his snug office in his cottage, he worried about Malory, pondered grades, and smiled at the little chipmunk that so often came to sit on his windowsill. Lately, the tiny creature had worked up the courage to come indoors. He'd discovered she loved toasted almonds, so he kept a bowl handy. He christened his wild friend "Li'l Darlin'" and spoke to her—it had to be a her—in soft low tones. Now, she abruptly hopped from the sill into the house and scampered across the floor, appearing on his desk, just out of reach, in the blink of an eye. He nudged the little bowl of almonds toward her. Sitting on her haunches, she picked one up and daintily began to nibble as she watched him work.

38

As the comforting scent of fireplaces began to fill the air more often by day and night, as green grass began to fade toward yellow or brown, Kendra and Samantha became close friends. They pored over Merilynn's journals and notes and endlessly studied her watercolors of the haunted town beneath Applehead Lake.

There had been no sign of Merilynn since the night the ghosts had come into their room—the phone call didn't count, both knew it was false. Still, Sam and Kendra chose to believe she was alive, that there was a chance of rescue, at least through Halloween night.

Between classes, they spent time in the library studying old newspaper articles and police reports, trying to glean clues from decades-old articles about missing or murdered students. They found that, often, girls went missing around certain dates; the solstices and equinoxes. May first and mid-August. And the last night of October.

"Halloween is the next time the ghost town is

supposed to come to life," Kendra mused. "That's good because when the town is alive, Holly Gayle walks. She and Eve will be among us."

"That's good," Sam murmured.

"They're on our side."

"They may be able to help us find Merilynn before it's too late."

"What if you're wrong?" Kendra asked suddenly. "What if Merilynn is already dead?"

"It's a chance worth taking, don't you think?"

"Yes." Tears formed in Kendra's eyes but she willed them away. It was a frustrating time; they had searched everywhere they could, looking for traces of their missing friend. On the weekend before Halloween, they even drove down into the Applehead Cheerleading Camp.

"Dear Lord," Kendra had said, seeing the shattered boathouse doors. The broken wood had been stacked near the dock and plywood had hastily been nailed up to cover the entrance, keeping the boats safe from mischievous college students and drunken fishermen.

They had examined the sand for footprints, but if there had been any left under the workmen's prints, the October zephyrs had erased them. Later that day, around noon, they had hiked to the knight's chapel, taking the route Sam remembered from so long ago, peering in the same window through which she had watched the sacrifice.

"Do you think they'll do it here?" Kendra asked, shivering with terror.

"Perform the sacrifice?" Sam walked boldly into the place that Kendra knew squeezed her heart and throat. She followed. All the grass looked the same;

they couldn't even find the place that had looked so sparse the time they came here during the night. "Yes," Sam finally said. "I think it's likely this is where they'll perform the sacrifice."

She spoke strongly, but Kendra could hear a faint tremble in her voice. "Let's get out of here, Sam. I don't think it's teaching us anything."

Kendra felt strange comfort in knowing that Sam hated this place as much as she did. Quickly, they left the building, but the terror didn't fade until they left the clearing as well. Both looked back at the chapel ruins, then looked at each other; they both knew they would be back soon but neither could voice it.

Instead, they went to Professor McCobb's office. He gently chastised Kendra for taking so long to visit him to have their chat about the Greenbriar Ghost. Over hot chocolate with marshmallows in the comfort of his book-lined office, they retraced the lore, comparing what they knew and what they read, looking for a truth. Eventually, charmed by the old man's white tangle of eyebrows, his lion's mane of wild white hair, and his cherubic lips, they even told him their theories.

None of it had seemed terribly real until he said he thought they might be right. Sitting in chairs opposite the old professor, Sam and Kendra took each other's hands. Both trembled almost uncontrollably.

39

The day faded. All Hallow's Eve arrived in Greenbriar. As twilight wrapped the campus in darkness, fraternity and sorority houses lit up, decorated with black and orange streamers, black cats, and ghosts. Jack-o'-lanterns sat plump and orange on the steps of the houses, carved faces grinning, fire in their eyes.

Gamma House had the most jack o'-lanterns. They lined the veranda railing, smiling, frowning, roaring, inscrutable, lusting. They sat one above the other on the steps to the house, gleaming and grinning their blazing eyes and smiles.

Most of the regular Gamma sisters would attend parties on campus or in town. Nearly all of them were currently at the small, relatively quiet celebration in Gamma House's great room, where sprays of dried roses no longer filled the fireplace. Instead, the huge maw was filled with blazing flames that licked hungrily at logs piled on the grate. On the marble fronting the huge fireplace, more carved pumpkins watched the festivities. Punch was poured. Sisters giggled. Young men laughed and spiked the punch.

Some partiers wore costumes, others did not, at least not yet. Parties in Gamma House were mild affairs; no one wanted to harm the furniture or the wallpaper, or knock over an antique lamp. After a warm up here, most of the girls would head out for the serious frat house parties.

At the moment, nearly all the Gamma sisters were in the great room. Obviously missing were most of the cheerleaders and the officers. *The Fata Morgana.* Thirteen.

And two more were out too, though they're lack of attendance wasn't noticed. Long before dark, Samantha and Kendra had slipped away, carrying bookbags filled with flashlights and weapons, water and first aid supplies.

McCobb had offered to help them in some way that none of the three had quite figured out. He had warned them of the danger, had told them that he had seen Malory before, had confirmed suspicions too absurd for Sam to even voice. But she had listened as he and Kendra spoke, and knew there would be no help. The Fata Morgana had Greenbriar University sewn up tight.

And the day before Halloween, Professor McCobb had stumbled and fractured his leg right after Sam and Kendra left his office after a long conversation. McCobb's secretary had explained that he would be in the hospital for a few days because they had to put a pin in his thigh. Then he would be recovering at home for a few weeks. Both girls suspected some sort of foul play—they had seen Malory watching them talk one day outside his classroom.

So, Sam and Kendra were all alone as they headed

for the chapel well before twilight. They spoke little, but exchanged lots of glances. Nervous ones.

There was still light in the sky when they reached the chapel's clearing. Keeping to the trees, they skirted it entirely, moving quietly until they reached the far side of the ruins, the side with the windows, not the wide doorway.

"We really ought to have more of a plan," Sam said as they examined a copse of close set pines as a possible hiding place. "Or at least some machine guns."

"Remember what McCobb said. The Forest Knight isn't our enemy. Or Merilynn's. We take our cues from her." Kendra paused, fingering the long letter opener in her pocket. "I sure wouldn't mind having one of those guns of Rambo's though."

"Me either. So, what do you think?" Sam snapped her wrist, causing Roddy, her tiny billy club, to grow with a reassuringly harsh metal-on-metal sliding sound. "We need to be able to see what's going on without being seen. This looks good to me."

"Me too."

Sam nodded and slipped off her backpack, pushing it up against some winter-burned ferns. Kendra followed suit. Soon, they were quietly settled on the forest floor, backs against the trees, puny weapons at hand and nearly no notion about what they were going to do.

"I can't believe we're doing this," Sam murmured.

"We have to."

"I know, but we're not prepared."

"You know what McCobb said. If Merilynn is what we think she is, she's prepared. We just need to be here to help her."

"Kendra, I hope you're right. If you're not, I'm afraid we're about to become just a couple more missing students in a long line of them."

Twilight settled in, shrouding them with dread as dark as their clothing. Time passed. A long time, agonizingly slow.

And then they heard voices on the other side of the chapel. Feminine voices, first just a couple; Malory and Heather. A bonfire crackled to life within the chapel walls. Alert, they listened, but the trees and snapping fire muffled the words. All they could be sure of was that the duo was lugging something heavy. Heather's curses rose over the other noises, and silenced the birds.

Merilynn? Kendra asked silently.

Sam could barely see her in the gloom. She shrugged, then whispered, "Maybe we should . . ."

She silenced as more voices neared. The Fata Morgana had arrived.

Holding a finger to her lips, she stood and peered through the trees, caught sight of dark-robed figures silhouetted in the flames.

40

Brittany arrived at the chapel late, infuriating her mistress, who threw her forest-colored cloak at her with barely a glance. Brittany stripped and pulled on the robe, discreetly wiping away signs of the sex she'd just had with Professor Tongue.

She had started seeing Tongue secretly nearly ten days ago. How could she possibly resist a man who was so kind to animals and to women. She'd spent hours sitting on his desk, watching his hands—nice artistic fingers, not terribly long, but strong and graceful—and finding herself more and more fascinated by the human. Drawn to him.

It began with an impulse blindly followed. After he had hand-fed her a honey-roasted almond, she skittered from the room, out the window, and not a minute later, knocked on his front door.

He'd opened it and simply stared at her.

"I'd do anything for some nuts," she said, unbuttoning her shirt to reveal her cleavage.

"I have nuts," he said hoarsely, then invited her in.

It was such fun, having him to herself, having a secret with him; she had told him Malory couldn't know about their secret affair, but he was smart enough to know that on his own. Thereafter, she began to visit him when she knew Malory was attending a class or riding a football player.

She felt affection for Tongue, the kind he probably felt for her chipmunk self, and that and the sex were gratifying, but she couldn't lie to herself; taking Malory's lover behind her back was equally gratifying. Especially now that she wasn't sure about Malory's suitability as a sorceress.

Brittany's dalliances with Tongue were heaven on earth, whatever the reasons behind them. Or at least they had been until an hour before when she had gotten carried away and suffocated the poor man with an extended orgasm the likes of which only an elemental could experience.

It was humiliating. It was embarrassing. And it had happened before. That was one of the reasons Malory wouldn't let her sample her human lovers in her absence. She knew Brittany could sexually murder a human male any number of ways. Usually, their hearts gave out. Tongue's lungs had burst because Brittany had stayed too long in the saddle, and by the time she realized her error, the man had been dead too long to bother reviving. He'd be nothing but a vegetable.

And Malory would be furious.

Brittany had dawdled after realizing her error, trying to decide what to do with the body. Malory would recognize magick. She finally decided to set fire to the cottage, then realized it would have to be done later; dusk was falling and Malory and the Fata

Morgana were waiting for her at the chapel. Professor Tongue would have to wait.

What would happen if she told Malory the truth? Fury, wrath, some nasty electrical bolts zapped her way. Brittany didn't need any of it, but she didn't fear it either. Especially now. Normally, a familiar didn't cross her sorcerer overtly, but times were changing. Tonight, if Malory pulled off the sacrifice, if Merilynn was truly out of the picture, things would probably go back to normal—or nearly normal. As long as Malory clung to the idea of sacrificing this particular daughter—more than half elemental, a truly special creature—Brittany couldn't trust her completely.

Now, she watched her mistress as she and her minions prepared for the sacrificial rites of All Hallow's Eve. Her eyes flashed dark and wild; even her movements were odd and jerky. Perhaps it was side effects from missing the last sacrifice, but Malory had grown more unstable and unrealistic over the last ten days. She was becoming an unsuitable mistress.

Something that most alarmed Brittany was the haphazard way her mistress had conducted the initiations of the new Fata Morganas. They were hurried and half-assed. Malory not only didn't teach them what they needed to know, but she chose her initiates badly. One she chose for her psychotic nature, for her willingness to kill her roommate over closet space. She was not Fata material; she was prison material. And the others? Simply warm bodies to fill slots. Brittany couldn't fault Malory too much there; there was no time to really choose. But those neophytes had no idea what was about to happen.

They didn't know they were about to take part in a sacrifice of any sort, let alone a human one, one of their lesser sisters. Malory's plan was to use magick to make them forget what they'd seen if they reacted badly, and her back-up plan was to kill them if magick didn't work. It was not how these things were done. It was wrong. *Wrong!*

Suddenly, Brittany itched for freedom for the first time in hundreds of years. She burned with desire for a new master or mistress. One who respected the Forest Knight. One who respected *her.*

41

Deep in the caverns on Applehead Island, Merilynn's body had lain, not dead, but in stasis, on a soft bed of living ferns by an underground brook, tended and healed by the Forest Knight until it was whole again and ready for her spirit to reenter.

Merilynn didn't want to return to the physical world. Here, with the Forest Knight, she had spent time in the Otherworld learning so much about the things she'd rarely even glimpsed while in her body, knowing things she'd only suspected. Here, she could see as she had never seen before. Here, her forest father schooled her in her power, *his* power, for it was born of him.

I don't want to leave you.

He looked at her with eyes similar to her own, and similar to those of her priestly father, who was also truly a son of the knight. The knight rarely spoke, but showed her pictures, and now he did both. Showing her an image of the ghostlights beneath the lake, of the amber lanterns in ghost houses and the brilliant stained glass of the old church, he told her, *You are always with me.*

I made a promise.

Yes.

May I return to you after?

You will know what to do. We are never apart. Go now. The fate of the living lies in your hands as well as the fate of the dead.

He sent her an image of Samantha and Kendra hiding behind the chapel, where a bonfire blazed. Where a victim waited for a sacrifice that the Forest Knight did not truly want. The knight had made this bargain long ago, and he would not dishonor it, Merilynn knew. But he would, in his own way, be glad to end it.

That night, Holly told me only I could stop Malory.

Then stop her now, before she snuffs out any more humans.

Merilynn slipped into her renewed body, felt blood pump, breathed in the air, felt it cool in her lungs, smelled its green scent, savored the babble of the brook. Sitting up, she cupped her hand in the fresh water and drank deeply.

"I'm alive!"

"Are you ready?" her father asked in a rumbly voice, part oak, part man.

"Yes."

"You will be able to hold your breath long enough to accomplish your task. Go now. Go and kill. Go and be free."

42

The ceremony began and Brittany, as always, stepped forward at Malory's signal and uncovered the sacrifice. Little Lou, the newest cheerleader, had been her mistress's pick despite the fact that she had many relatives that would inquire and cause problems for them.

It was just another example of Malory's lack of judgment. She didn't care about the problems that would arise, no more than she cared about the current Fata Morganas. As cold as Malory had always been, she had still been loyal to her Fata Morganas, taking care of them, nurturing them, teaching them what they needed to know.

But when Brittany had made a remark about her lack of thought about the Fatas, Malory had shaken the comment off like it was a gnat, telling her familiar that they didn't matter since she and Brittany would be leaving Greenbriar soon.

They had left this place many times before, but she had always cared. She always put this, her favorite of all the Fata Morgana groups, in the hands of her most trusted lieutenants. But only months from leaving Gamma House, she hadn't even discussed replacements with Brittany.

Bound and gagged, Lou's eyes betrayed her terror as she stared up into Brittany's own.

Though she didn't truly care about Lou any more than she would about a wounded bird—less actually—Brittany found herself unable to meet the victim's gaze as she fastened her to the spikes driven into the ground and secured by a small spell when Malory first arrived.

She went about her business, her heart cold, making sure that Lou could not roll out of the way of Malory's black onyx ceremonial dagger.

The chanting began, led by Heather while Malory sang an eerie counterpoint spell. Brittany joined in because that was what a familiar did, but she watched the new Fata Morganas, the initiates, seeing anxiety and fear on the faces of all but the psychotic one. That bitch licked her lips as she stared at the naked, helpless girl laid out before her.

The chanting continued.

43

Merilynn dived into the underground pool of water, swimming like a fish, quickly clearing the cavern and island to glide rapidly deeper and deeper, heading for the ghost town beneath the black water.

She flashed through the water, holding her breath without any effort, seeing as she saw only when in spirit form. Before her, Applehead began to wink to life, more and more lights blossoming amber as she approached.

They're welcoming me. She reached the town, moving quickly among the buildings, seeing near-mindless ghosts holding their lanterns, seeing others, spirits, not just ghosts, gathering before her, lighting her way. In some of the old buildings, ghosts seemed to go through the motions of dining or reading. One stoked an amber fire under a cookpot.

She found the church and swam inside, looking sadly at the scattering of bones from Malory's victims. *So many.* Had Malory willed them here through magick because of some perversely twisted sense of humor? Had Holly used the currents to pull them

into the sanctuary? Merilynn saw a closed door behind the altar and pulled it open, exposing a small
room. The perfect bodies of Holly Gayle and Eve
Camlan sat together, arms and hair entwined, Eve's
head upon Holly's breast. Merilynn hesitated, then
moved closer.

No. Come to the steeple.

Holly's voice.

Leave them. Close the door. They are safe there.

Merilynn glided back into the church and found
the staircase to the steeple. She swam upward toward
the gleaming jewels of stained glass that depicted the
village of Applehead before it was covered by the
lake.

Holly and Eve waited for her beside it. Merilynn
smiled at them, then Holly pointed at a rectangle of
emerald glass. Merilynn saw the small sword, fitted
along the rectangle to look like one more piece of
leading. But the sword shown silver and as she
grasped the hilt, the green gemstone bloomed under
her touch. Wonderingly, she turned the sword in her
hand. The blade was long enough to stop a heart's
beat, and the stone was so large that it had the same
faceted brilliance on each side of the hasp. Nothing
filtered its brilliance.

Hurry! There's no time!

Merilynn looked at Holly and Eve and nodded.
Then, using the sword to light her way, she swam
across the lake more swiftly than any human could
even imagine.

44

Chants rose to fever pitch. Magick sparked the air, filled it until it crackled like the fire itself. Malory began to lift off the ground, feet dangling. Brittany was swept up as well, and their robes fell away. The experienced Fatas levitated next, boosted by Malory and Brittany, and as they rose, their robes swept off their gleaming bodies as if taken by the wind. The initiates, all but untrained, stayed earthbound, but even their robes fell away, caught in the magick, obeying the power of all.

Brittany loved the feeling of the electricity in the atmosphere. She tasted the air, but felt no sign of the Forest Knight's presence, realizing she had yet to hear his cry.

But she sensed something else nearby.

Something different. Something powerful. Something exciting. It was almost here. Eagerly she scanned, but she saw nothing.

Yet.

45

Merilynn burst out of the lake, running onto the sand, pausing to take deep breaths of fresh air. She smelled the lake and the forest, and a bonfire. She smelled magick too.

From the time spent with the knight in spirit form, she knew the forest intimately. She could see unnaturally well, too. So, hiding the brilliance of the green gem and silvery sword beneath her wet jacket, she ran, as fleet as her father, toward the chapel.

She silently came to rest in the shadows of the chapel, just outside one of the windows at the rear. Crouching, she cautiously peered inside and watched the circle of thirteen robed figures. A bonfire burned.

"Merilynn!"

She whipped her head around, saw Sam and Kendra in nearby shadows, just as the knight had shown her. She put her finger to her lips. *Silence!*

46

As Malory Thomas floated to the ground and stepped forward to kneel beside her sacrifice, Merilynn began to murmur the old words of power that the Forest Knight had taught her. They were words older than Malory's, older than any human's language. As she said them, she unsheathed the sword and the stone.

Green brilliance lit up the night. The chanting stopped. Behind her, she heard Sam and Kendra gasp, but she paid no attention. Instead, she threw her head back and yelled the banshee cry her father had taught her. The sound shook the ground, made the wind blow, brought birds out of nests.

Merilynn leaped through the window, ran through the bonfire, untouched, holding the sword high.

Malory, her onyx dagger raised to take the heart from her victim, looked up just as Merilynn landed on her, toppling her backward and plunging the sword deeply into her mother's breast.

Into her heart.

Malory flailed and cried for her familiar, but no help came.

Green brilliance flared as the weapon claimed Malory's life and power and fed it into the Forest Knight's own daughter.

Merilynn pushed Malory's body to the ground, withdrawing the sword, then rising and holding it up into the night, she called. "Father! Here is your sacrifice!"

She let out another earth-shattering cry then yanked up Malory Thomas's head and sliced her head off as if it were a wing off a fly. Holding it by the hair, she turned, displaying it to all of Malory's followers. "Your queen is dead. Morgana is gone from this world!"

Sam and Kendra moved in, untying Lou and giving her a robe. Merilynn barely noticed. She threw a binding spell to keep all of the Fata Morganas within the chapel until she could deal with them. Then she smiled at Sam and Kendra and little Lou.

She touched Lou's forehead and murmured, "Forget." The girl, dazed to begin with, looked like she was asleep on her feet.

Then Merilynn threw her head back and gave a shout of triumph, frightening in its strength, but not its tone. Silence followed. One second, two, three. Then she smiled as her father's great answer of triumph sounded from his island.

She basked in power and pleasure for one long moment, then turned to see Kendra and Sam staring at her. Behind them, Fata Morganas sat or stumbled, dazed and confused, unable to leave.

"Hey, guys," she said to her friends. "How are things in the real world?"

Before either could reply, a chipmunk suddenly

raced up to her and stood on its hind legs, little paws clasped as if in prayer.

"Hello, little one." Merilynn bent and extended her hand to the animal. It ran up her arm and perched on her shoulder, nuzzling her. She smiled at Sam and Kendra. "It looks like I've just made a new friend."

December

47

A fire crackled merrily in the great room of Gamma House, and before the windows that looked out over the night-shrouded back lawn, a huge Monterey pine stood ten feet tall, majestic in its raiment of twinkling white lights and globes that looked like the most delicate confections of spun silver and gold. Topping the Yule tree was a sparkling shooting star.

Most of the sisters of Gamma House were here this Sunday night, gathered together and apart, deep in books, outlining, highlighting, taking notes for the exams that would plague them during the coming week.

Kendra, curled in the corner of a love seat, notebook in hand, looked around the room. The house felt different now, homier, more comfortable and welcoming. The departure of Malory Thomas and Brittany was the reason. Without them here, things actually felt sisterly. She smiled, jotted down a stray thought, and fell into reverie once more.

Things had changed, but remained much the

same. Merilynn had taken instant and unquestioned charge of the Fata Morganas. All of them had obeyed her on All Hallow's Eve, and continued to do so now, even though she was rarely here.

Merilynn had changed in her time on the island with the Forest Knight. *Her father.* She roamed the woods at all hours, long and lithe, red hair flying as she moved among the trees, the little chipmunk nearly always riding her shoulder or frolicking at her heels.

One day Kendra asked her about the friendly striped creature, if it was really a chipmunk or something more, something very familiar. Merilynn had only smiled in her fey way, giving an answer with her eyes that Kendra could not translate.

Merilynn's slightly flaky personality had changed very much. She was still friendly but far away. No one feared her, except perhaps the Fata Morganas that she hadn't sent away.

Sent away. How she had sent them, and where, were two questions that, for now, Kendra didn't want an answer for. Merilynn was the daughter of a good priest, a powerful forest god, and what had to be one of the wickedest mothers of all time. Kendra studied her friend often, seeing the calm power behind her smile. She wondered how she used the power. How she would use it in years to come.

Some day I'll write a book about a forest queen.

Kendra had the room to herself; Merilynn had moved into Malory's suite, and was less easy to know now. Although she invited her friends to her lush room to watch movies and eat popcorn or down the occasional margarita, she was . . . *What is she?* Kendra stared at the ceiling a moment, then wrote down the answer: *A force of nature.* She also had a handsome boyfriend now, most often seen after he was already in the house, walking with her down the halls, disappearing into her rooms for hours. Handsome, tanned, with thick blond hair and deep blue eyes, Brandon was hard-muscled and compact, standing an inch shorter than Merilynn herself. Neither seemed to notice. When he was around, which was more and more, Mcrilynn's smile sparkled even brighter than usual. They were a match made, if not in heaven, then someplace very similar, but greener.

Kendra heard the entry door being opened—holiday bells jingled arrivals and departures. A little thrill ran through her.

"Kendra," a soft male voice said from the doorway.

She closed her notebook and stood, then turned and beamed at Jimmy Freeman. Merilynn wasn't the only one who had found a friend of the opposite sex. She walked to the threshold and tilted her head up for a quick meeting of the lips.

"So, are you going to tell me what your big surprise is?" he asked.

"No. I'm going to show you. Let me go get my coat and flashlights."

His face split in a broad, mellow smile that melted her. They had yet to consummate the relationship and the tension was constantly tight, constantly delicious. He called it foreplay and seemed to relish waiting for the right time and place.

"I'll be right back." Kendra trotted up the stairs and unlocked her room. She shrugged on her warmest coat and grabbed her knapsack, pulled out her flashlight and checked the batteries. They looked strong, but she dropped an extra set in the bottom of the bag and placed the light itself in a pocket on the jacket. To the backpack, she added two bottles of water and a pair of ruby-red apples, wrapped in a towel to keep them from bruising. *No.* Smiling to herself, picturing Jimmy waiting for her at the foot of the stairs, she plucked the velvety blanket throw from the foot of her bed, folded it again and put it in the bag, then placed the apples in the deep fold and tucked the blanket in around them.

She closed the pack and clicked the latch, then swung it around and shrugged it on. Jimmy would insist on carrying it and be pleasantly surprised when he found out how little it weighed. Kendra glanced around the room, ready to leave, then paused, returned to her desk, and took the letter opener from it, slipping it into the long inner pocket of her coat, where it joined her pepper spray.

Satisfied now, she turned off the light and flipped the lock on the knob and left the room. Seeing Jimmy, she took the stairs two at a time.

Eyeing the bulging pack, he asked, "Are we going camping?"

"In December?" She laughed.

"Hey, it's California, after all. No snow."

"California. Not Hawaii." She grinned at him. "You still have a lot to learn about this place."

Jimmy, from Vermont, returned the grin. "Feels like Hawaii to me."

They walked outside. The cold wind washed over Kendra's face. "Jimmy, trust me, this isn't Hawaii. They grow apples up here. Apples need a cold winter. And for your information, once in a while it really does snow here."

"Don't try to one-up me on snow, Kendra. I've got you beat on that and you know it."

They walked down the paving beside the reflecting pool, and down to the roadside in front of the house, where his weird little motor-scooter—*more guts than a scooter, but not a good statement about penis size,* he'd told her—waited. He handed her a helmet and donned his own. He got on first; then she tucked in behind him, moving up close, putting her arms around him, hanging on tight just because she wanted to.

"Where to?"

"The lake."

His head swiveled. "The *what?*"

"Applehead Lake, by way of the old chapel. It's not a bad hike, just a quarter mile in."

"That's a dangerous spot. It's haunted."

"I know, Jimmy. I was the one who told you all the stories, remember?"

"You and Professor McCobb. What are you doing, taking us there? You want to see some ghosts, or maybe a serial killer?"

"No serial killer, but I'd be happy to see some ghosts."

"What about the Greenbriar Ghost?"

"He prefers to be called the Forest Knight. Merilynn told me."

"The funny red-haired girl?"

"That's her."

"So she's tight with the knight?"

"Very. If we run into him, be respectful. And don't leave litter in his chapel. Merilynn says he hates that."

"You're nuts," he said, trying to catch her kiss. It landed on his helmet.

"I'm just messing with you, Jimmy. We're meeting some friends and we're going to see a show."

"Okay. As long as you protect me from the ghosts, I'll follow you to the ends of the earth. And even to that haunted lake." He paused. "Hey, we aren't going out in a boat, are we?"

"Too cold. We'll do that some other time."

"You're the boss." The engine didn't roar as he turned it on, but it purred pretty impressively. "Hang on tight."

"I will."

48

Samantha Penrose walked alone, the greenish gleam of a light-stick and a brilliant half-moon giving her enough light to travel the path to the Knight's chapel.

Since All Hallow's Eve, she had taken this path many times, by night and by day, relishing what she once feared, hoping to see the knight as he was now. Not as he had been when she witnessed the sacrifice nearly a decade ago.

That was what she had forgotten. Merilynn, new and improved, had helped her remember. She knew now that the Fata Morganas had fled after the sacrifice, leaving the chapel even before the knight's angry shriek filled the air and shook the trees. The high priestess—Malory—took the dead girl's heart with her as she hurried away. A moment later, the banshee howl came again, closer, arriving in a hurricane wind that came crashing down into the chapel.

Sam had cringed in the shadows, but still peered through the window. The wind had spun around a greenish figure that covered the girl's body for a minute, maybe less, then rose. She'd seen the flash of the knight's green eyes as they spotted her.

And she expected to die.

Now, she stepped into the clearing onto the remains of last spring's grass. The wards had been lifted, Merilynn had explained shortly after Halloween. It was a holy place, not a forbidden place. Her eyes had darkened as she spoke, saying that anyone thickheaded enough to defile the place would likely pay a price.

Sam didn't question her. She understood. She had seen what Merilynn had metamorphosed into in the chapel on the last night of October. It wasn't a story that Sam would ever report in *Time* magazine, or *Newsweek*. It was a story meant for Kendra to tell. It was folklore in the making. *An urban legend now, folklore later. It has to age.*

Kendra had been horrified that night, traumatized, but she and Merilynn had spent many hours talking about it with her. And Merilynn had done something, laying her hands on Kendra's head, speaking softly as she moved her fingers in small circles over her forehead and cheeks. Kendra had relaxed—Sam had relaxed just watching and listening, for that matter—and then fallen asleep. When she awoke half an hour later, the terror had drained away. She was her old self again.

Now, at the chapel's threshold, Samantha hesitated only an instant, then stepped inside. The air seemed warmer, tingling with electricity.

"Forest Knight," Sam whispered, as she always did when she came here. "Please, show yourself to me."

The air wavered, warming around her, filled with the scent of summer pine and ferny grottoes. It nearly overwhelmed her. Her ears felt pressure and popped and the air seemed gone from her lungs. And then a whirlwind grew before her, twirling up from the ground itself, growing taller, until it towered over her. The scent of the forest filled her senses, but the wind didn't touch her. Suddenly green eyes blinked to brilliant life only inches from her own. The wind vanished and before her stood the Forest Knight, at least seven feet tall, even though he held his head in his big hands, dangling it in front of her nose by its leafy hair.

Frightened, she said meekly, "Hello."

The green face spread into a grin; then the mouth opened and hearty laughter blew hot desert air into her face.

"For you," rumbled the mouth in the severed head. His other hand held out a bright spring of holly with brilliant red berries.

Then he was gone. Just. Like. That.

Gathering her nerves, she walked out of the chapel and straight into the beam of a flashlight. Instinctively, her hand drew the metal nightstick from her pocket.

"It's me."

"Kendra! I'm so glad to see you! Hi Jimmy." She tried to control herself, but it was impossible. "I saw him!"

"Him?" Kendra asked.

"Him." Sam showed her the holly spring. "And now I know where Merilynn got her sense of humor. Come on, let's get to the lake; then I'll tell you the rest."

49

The trio saw flashes of light between the trees as they neared the lake, but when they emerged from the forest and saw the city on the water, they were speechless.

Sam took in the city of castles and towers, spirals and pillars, arches, balconies, vast mullioned windows of colored glass lit like jewels. Amber lights glowed from within the pale whites and tans, misty blues and delicate rose-tinted structures. "What is it?" she murmured.

"I don't know, but it's sure not Applehead, risen from the bottom of the lake," Kendra told her.

"It's amazing," Jimmy said. "Is this what you brought me to see?"

Kendra chuckled. "No. I brought you here to watch a meteor shower."

The three glanced up at the velvet dark sky.

"The knight told me to tell you that you're very brave."

Sam's heart lurched and she whirled. "Merilynn, I *hate* it when you do that."

Merilynn's laughter lilted. She was dressed in dark green and her chipmunk was perched on her shoulder nibbling a nut. "I'm sorry." She took the arm of the fiftyish man standing next to her. "You remember my father, Martin, don't you?"

"Of course," Kendra said. She stepped forward and hugged the man.

Sam shook his hand. "I'm glad to see you again." Martin smiled. "And you."

"Jimmy, this is Merilynn's daddy, Martin. Merilynn, you've met Jimmy?"

"No, actually." She clasped his hand and said, "I hear we were pretty hot and heavy though."

"What?"

"Relax, Jimmy," Kendra said. "She's pulling your leg."

"Not entirely," Sam said.

"What are you talking about?" Jimmy asked.

"Nothing important," Sam told him.

But he no longer looked at Merilynn. Now his eyes were fixed on Martin's neck. On the collar visible just in the V of his jacket. "That doesn't look like a white T-shirt," he ventured.

"It's not."

"He's a priest."

"Not all priests are pedophiles," Martin said gently. "And some aren't even gay. Not that there's anything wrong with that." He smiled and looked at the lake. "I always knew my little girl was an artist."

Sam turned, horrified that she had forgotten about the ghostly castles sitting on the water, seeming to cast their reflection down into the depths of the lake. "It's amazing, Merilynn. Astonishing."

"What is it?" Kendra asked.

"My other father taught me the trick. It's a real but rare phenomenon I thought you two would be interested in, so I whipped it up. It's a mirage."

"The Fata Morgana mirage?"

"Yes, Sam. I thought you'd like to see one while you can."

They gazed at it for long moments, no one speaking. Finally, Kendra spoke. "It's beautiful."

"As Malory was long ago. It's named for her. Morgana, sister to Arthur. Betrayer of the king and her mentor. She had a long reign." Merilynn fell silent.

"Why did you say you wanted us to see the mirage while we can?"

Merilynn smiled. "I wondered how long it would take you to ask. It's because I won't be able to make such a huge glamour again after tonight. Power turned Malory into a demon. I don't want that. Perhaps some day I'll feel capable of handling power wisely, but for now . . ." She paused, unzipping her jacket and pulling the small broadsword with its brilliant gleaming stone. "For now, I'm returning this to a safe place. Look at the water."

Slowly, Holly Gayle emerged from the water, not walking toward them but moving straight up until she seemed to stand on it. In her long white gown, she looked like a lady from the castles far beyond.

Sam gasped as the spirit glided toward them. Merilynn stepped to the water's edge, holding the gleaming blade across her palms. The jewel sent out a light of its own.

Sam hesitated, them moved to Merilynn's side. The others followed. Holly looked from person to person, her eyes radiating happiness. Out of the corner of her eye, Sam saw movement and then Eve stood there with them, smiling, happy again.

"Take this back to the church for safekeeping for me, Holly. Will you do this for me?"

Of course.

Holly put her hands out and Merilynn put the miniature sword in them. Power filtered from her and into the spirit. "You are all free now," she said. "I was afraid you might have gone already."

We don't wish to leave now that Malory is gone.

We're staying, Eve said inside Sam's head. *As long as you are here, we will be.*

Merilynn's smile was radiant. "But why?"

We're no longer bound to the lake. We can do as we please. And it is our pleasure to guard you. And to keep this safe for you. She gazed at the sword. Holly bowed her head to Merilynn, then slowly glided backward and then down into the lake.

Sam watched the light of the gemstone until it was lost. She looked back up at the mirage, but it was rapidly fading away. "It was so beautiful."

"It was," Merilynn said. "But so are other things. Look up!"

Meteors burst like distant fireworks above them and a deep rumbling vibrated the ground, then raised in pitch. It was the Forest Knight's jolly laughter.

Please turn the page for an exciting sneak peek of

Tamara Thorne's

next novel

THUNDER ROAD

coming in July 2004 from Pinnacle Books!

PROLOGUE

April

The last things Madge Marquay saw were the balls of light darting across the night sky.

How long ago? Hours? Days? A week or more? she couldn't be sure in this unending darkness. All she knew was that after working late at Madland, she had strolled out to the amusement park's apparently deserted parking lot and paused by her car to breathe in the crisp desert air. Then she glanced up at the midnight sky, at the brilliant dusting of stars.

She had heard about the lights from friends and neighbors, but it was the first time she'd actually seen them. The orbs were amazing, simultaneously magnificent and frightening, as they cavorted above the stark silhouettes of the Madelyn Mountains, flashing in and out of existence at whim. Suddenly she understood why no one who had seen them believed they were aircraft from the military bass, weather balloons, or ball lightning.

Madge had been easy prey for her attacker as she stood, mesmerized, staring at the sky, wishing Henry were here with her. Suddenly someone had grabbed her from behind and clamped a chloroformed rag over her nose and mouth.

And then, nothing. Now she wondered if the strange lights would be the last things she would ever see.

She could hear the tourists, but she couldn't make them hear her. Madge Marquay, bound, gagged, and blindfolded, lay somewhere below the Haunted Mine Ride in a cold rocky room that reeked of death, in a darkness so thick that it seemed to clog her lungs. Far above, one of the little mine trains rumbled by, and she moaned around her gag, trying to free a scream that could no more escape her lips than she could the mining pit.

Tears ran down her cheeks as utter silence resumed. Henry had to be looking for her, had to be worried, but would he ever think to walk the old passages on their own property, to climb down the ancient iron ladders to find her here in a pit dug and abandoned 130 years ago? She'd be a fool if she believed he would. Henry, their friends, and the police would search the canyons and mountains, they would look behind rocks and in brush-clogged drainage ditches, just as they had when Kyla Powers vanished a month ago.

But they never found her, or Joe Huxley, for that matter. But Madge thought she knew where they were. Down here with her. Despite the chill, she could smell death all around her. It was not an odor that numbed her sense of smell, but one that grew stronger, breeding sick panic in her gut.

She lay there, slowly being hypnotized by the dark, by her thirst and hunger, barely aware of the searing pain in her arm where her captor had peeled away her flesh. Her mind drifted, escaping to the past, to the time nearly fifteen years ago when she and Henry had leased the old Moonstone Silver Mine from the Country Parks Department and turned it into the biggest and best attraction in Old Madelyn.

They rigged music to play in different parts of the ride, using the *Grand Canyon* Suite for the tame vistas, "Night on Bald Mountain" for the runaway train sections and "In the Hall of the Mountain King" for the huge central showcase, a room containing treasure boxes filled with gold-painted rocks that were guarded by Disneyesque dwarfs and presided over by an imposing golden-haired king on his throne. It wasn't perfect, or even terribly original, but it was the product of their labor and they loved it. It was their dream.

Shoring up the dirty old mine, making it safe, then running the wiring and track for the passenger cars had been Henry's job, while Madge did art and design in her spare hours. As a history teacher, she loved digging into the books of Irish mining lore and turning the tales into figures and images to delight and frighten visitors. The stories had become so vivid to her that, in her mind's eye, she could see the dwarfs sneaking up on an unwary human miner, their pickaxes ready to strike.

Another train rumbled overhead, bringing reality with it. She moaned around the filthy rag between her teeth, felt the tears coursing down her cheeks and wished to God she could suck them into her mouth. She was so thirsty. So very thirsty.

PART ONE

Tales of the New West

Perhaps they have always been here. On earth. With us.

—Jacques Vallee, *Dimensions*

. . . Make straight in the desert a highway for our God.

—Isaiah 40:3

I will be disappointed if they [UFOs] turn out to be nothing more than advanced space-craft.

—Jacques Vallee, *Confrontations*

TUESDAY

1

Tom Abernathy

Sheep, thought Tom Abernathy, *damned, stupid sheep.* He hopped down into the runoff ditch to avoid getting caught in the mass of wool coming up behind him, thinking that these days he spent a good portion of his time avoiding one sort of flock or another.

Soon they were everywhere, Christly dirty, dust-kicking sheep, before and behind him, chewing and bahing, stinking and shitting, filling Thunder Road and trampling the orange and yellow wildflowers for twenty yards to the north. Marie, whom he had yet to glimpse, wasn't so bad (quite the opposite, as a matter of fact), though she usually smelled of lanolin and dip, which Tom supposed was a fitting perfume for a lady sheepherder. Truth be told, for two years now that aroma, combined with the soft, sweet scent of Marie's skin and hair, had intoxicated him.

He wasn't unique: A lot of the men in town were smitten by Marie. While Abernathy kept his yearnings to himself, Phil, the morning counterman at Ray's Truck Stop Café, down in New Madelyn, was so in love with her that she could have smelled like owl shit and swamp water and he wouldn't have cared a bit. Phil's courtship consisted simply of serenading her with "I Get a Kick Out of Ewe" whenever she came in for coffee; not particularly original, but not bad for the likes of New Madelyn, and Marie didn't seem to mind. Men working at Madland, which was what you called Old Madelyn Historic Park if you were employed there, were a bit more creatively uncouth in their comments, which included such songs as "Marie Had a Little Ram" and questions along the lines of "Ewe want me, Marie? I want ewe." Franklin Hank Flinn, the Owner of the octopus—Flinn called it the octopussy because he liked to be dirty—once asked Marie about the longevity of ram erections, and that was the only time anyone could ever remember seeing the sheepherder lose her temper. For such a tiny woman, she had astoundingly strong hands, and Frank Hank swore that with one quick grab and twist, she'd almost removed the source of his happiness forever.

Tom sneezed, sucking in dust, coating his teeth with the stuff. "Goddamned sheep," he grunted, pulling a faded red bandanna from his back pocket. He flipped it, folded it crosswise, and tied it over this nose and mouth *bandido*-style. He loved doing that as much now, at the ripe old age of forty-two, as he had when he was just a little stick of a kid. For good measure, he tilted the brim of his brown beaver felt Stetson down a little.

"Hey, cowboy!" Marie's voice, clear as birdsong, rose above the bahing of the sheep.

Aiming for nonchalance, he halted and glanced up. "How you doin', Marie?" Squinting, he pushed the hat brim a little lower against the bright spring sun.

"Doing good." She swung off Rex, her raven black gelding, and let one rein fall. Dorsey, one of her border collies, made to grab it, but she stopped him with a meaningful glance. Tail down, he quickly rejoined his partner, Wild Bill. "Get back to work, you two," Marie told the dogs as she joined Tom in the trench. "Come," she told the horse, and he obediently moved two steps closer to the dry canal and waited to follow wherever she might go.

She sure has a way with animals, Tom thought, catching her scent. "Bright out today."

"That's why they call it the desert."

"You're a smart-ass woman, you know that?" He wondered how she kept the dust off her teeth.

"I know it, cowboy."

Marie Lopez had light olive skin and big chocolate eyes, and if she had favored bright skirts and cheap jewelry rather than Levi's and chambray shirts, and if she let her wavy dark hair flow loose instead of keeping it tied back under a straw cowboy hat, she would have made a great gypsy.

He ran his tongue over his teeth to clean off any remaining dust, then pulled the kerchief down around his neck. "So why don'tcha give up these stinkin' sheep and read fortunes at Madland?" he asked for maybe the thousandth time.

"Because I like to make an *honest* living," she replied for maybe the five hundredth time. She had about another five hundred answers, all different, all colorful and pleasantly obscene, and that's why he asked her the same question so often.

"You sayin' Carlo ain't honest?" Disappointment at being handed the stock answer made him feel feisty.

She cocked her head and drilled him with her eyes, but he didn't do anything except let a calculated smile crack his long, leathery face.

She grunted. "When I look at you like that, you're supposed to tuck your tail between your legs and run like hell, Abernathy."

"I am?" the smile widened.

"You're okay," she said, dead serious. "You don't spook."

He nodded, determined to start something. "Carlo don't spook either, but you write him off because of his dishonest profession."

"Quit trying to yank my chain, cowboy. Carlo's a shrink in gypsy's clothing. He doesn't do anything but make people feel good."

That was true. The Madland fortune teller and Marie were a lot alike: smart, hard to figure, and moody as hell, which was probably why he liked them. Carlo Pelegrine, like the shepherdess, spent a lot of time fending off the opposite sex. The only woman who seemed unaffected by Carlo's moody good looks was Marie, and Tom occasionally worried that their similarities would pull them together, cutting him out of the race before he even got around to getting into it. And most likely, he thought, his teasing them only worsened the odds.

"Tom?"

"Yep?"

"Why aren't you riding today?"

He shrugged, "Belle's getting new shoes right now." The pure truth was, he could have taken one of the other horses, but he'd been in need of the kind of peace and quiet that anything made of flesh and blood, except his favorite mare, would disrupt. He needed to be alone to think: Things were on the wind. He smiled grimly. Things besides sheep.

"You were walking along so slow, Tom," she persisted. "What were you thinkng about?"

He kicked a dried-up horse potato with the toe of his boot and drawled, "Oh, about that time you nearly twisted Franklin Hank's wiener off."

Her delighted laughter do-re-mi'd down the scale. Everything about Marie was musical. "I love it when you talk dirty, cowboy."

"You sure didn't love it when Franklin Hank talked dirty."

"There's a difference. He's a dirty old man."

"He's not much older than me."

"Oh, don't play stupid, Abernathy. There's ten-year-olds who are dirty old men. They're born, not made. Frank Flinn's a dirty old man, and no natural woman can abide him. He's dirty even when he's clean. Even his eyes are dirty. And that slimy old voice. Flinn could ask a woman to go to church with him and end up slapped."

They walked along awhile longer, jumping rapidly from subject to subject because Marie was taking the flock a couple miles north to graze in Rattlesnake Canyon and they wouldn't get to chat again for a week or so.

With all the weirdos acting up lately, Tom wished she wouldn't go out on the range by herself, but he knew better that to say so. Instead, he told her about the ribbons two of his horses won last week in the barrel races in Victorville, and then they shot a little shit about the new expanded stunt show that had been drawing the tourists to Madland on the weekends. By the time the ditch ran out, they'd also covered self-proclaimed prophet James Robert Sinclair, who insisted that the apocalypse was now, the latest UFO sightings, most of them by Janet Wister's Space Friends club, and Franklin Hank's aborted attempt to seduce Frannie Holder, Tom's horse trainer. (Rumor had it, she'd stuck her riding crop where the sun didn't shine, but he doubted it since Frank hank would like that sort of thing.)

"Well, here's where I head for the hills." Marie swung herself up into Rex's saddle. "Time to get the flock out of here," she added, smirking. She whistled and, when the dogs came running, she raised her arm and pointed toward the hills. "Dorsey, Bill, turn!"

The collies barked once, in unison, then took off, beginning to shift the direction of the flock.

"Amazing," Tom said. "I bet you could train crows if you had a mind to."

"Thanks, but I can't take the credit. The boys are smart." She smiled gently, watching them work. "Guess I'll see you in a week or so, Tom."

He shivered despite the warm spring sunshine. *Devil just walked on my grave.* "You be careful up there, Marie. Don't let any snakes in your bedroll."

"Don't worry. I'm leaving Franklin Hank down here with you." She turned the horse, ready to follow the flock.

"Marie?"

"Yeah?"

"Those sheep you lost last month . . . You really think a mountain lion got them?"

"I haven't found a better explanation." She paused. "Why?"

"Watch out, okay?"

"Aren't you an old worrywart today? Sure, I'll watch out for the kitty. But I'll be fine. the boys sleep right beside me and the rifle's on my pack, see?"

"The Space Friends think space aliens carved 'em up, so you better watch out for little blue men, too."

"Little blue men are better than no men at all." she gave him an indecipherable look. "See you later, cowboy."

"See you, Marie."

He stood there in the middle of Thunder Road, watching until she and her sheep were nothing more than specks against the jagged red hills. He shivered, despite the warmth, the hairs prickling up on the back of his neck again. "You be careful, girl," he whispered, and started walking again.

His worrying worried him as much as anything. Tom took great pride and satisfaction in his tranquil nature, as well as in the fact that his laconic cowboy act wasn't much of an act at all: It had become a way of life. "You'll never amount to anything, son, if you don't get out there and compete," his dad had often told him. His father, who had graduated at the head of his class from Harvard, had gone on to become one of the most respected cardiologists in the country. For a man like that, to be stuck with a son who dropped out of college, had no interest in medicine or, worse yet, football, who wanted nothing more than to own a horse and be a cowboy, had to have been the ultimate trial.

He smiled to himself. His dad, though incapable of understanding him, had always accepted him, more or less, and could actually respect him now. He'd begun referring to Tom as a breeder of champion quarter horses ten years before that held a lick of truth. Possibly his father's stories planted the idea in Tom's head, or possibly not, but either way, it was a good excuse to surround himself with horses instead of being content with just one. However it had happened, now Tom had a dozen prizewinners (the horses being far more competitive than Tom himself) and they brought in sizable amounts of money, allowing him to pay their trainer, Ms. Frannie Holder (also far more competitive than he) very well to keep them in top form. With Frannie doing the dirty work, Tom was free to spend much of his time at Madland, where he lassoed and did some fancy shooting in the stunt show, taught city kids about the burros and farm animals in the petting zoo, or simply sat around shooting the bull with Carlo or the stunt show people or anyone who happened to be handy.

He indulged in other pleasures as well. During spring and fall, the main tourist seasons, he often rode down to the campground to tell a few ghost stories around the campfire. And just about every week, he had company over to his big open-beamed ranch house with built-in and central everything. People loved to visit, but whether they came for the company, the air-conditioning, or his ranch manager's skill with a charbroiler—Davy Styles could barbecue a vulture and make it taste good—Tom didn't really know or care.

But his favorite thing to do was to ride into the Madelyn Mountains with nothing but his bedroll, guitar, and cooking supplies. Sometimes he'd go into Spirit Canyon, at the east end of Thunder Road, where the hills were so chock-full of mineral deposits that at sunset they glowed with copper greens and ferrous reds and purples. Other times he traveled due north, taking the trail that Marie was on now, over the hills and down into Rattlesnake Canyon, a starkly beautiful, eerily isolated area full of Joshua trees and mesquite. Wherever he landed, he'd build a campfire, then pick bad guitar and croon out of earshot of everything but the coyotes. After that, he'd lie back and count the stars, all by his lonesome.

Marie's alone out there. The goose bumps stood up once more, and as he glanced north, he hoped she was right in thinking that a mountain lion had been responsible for the attacks. He wasn't so sure.

For one thing, the kills he'd heard about sounded too neat; carnivores made a mess. If an animal died of natural causes and nothing got at the body but insects and birds, you sometimes got that neatness. There was nothing like dry air and a hill full of ants to cause the clipped and missing organs and incision-like inroads in the flesh that had the UFO nuts hollering Interstellar Surgeons! and Jim Bob Sinclair and his flock of faithful crying Satan! just as loud.

And then there were the disappearances. In the last three months, as many locals had vanished without a trace. While it was true that Joe Huxley occasionally took off unannounced for a few weeks or even a month when the prospecting bug bit him, this time he'd been gone since February. His Jeep was still in his carport and there was no sign of him at his claims in the Madelyns or Spirit Canyon.

Then, late in March, Kyla Powers closed up her

leather shop one night and disappeared into thin air. Maybe she'd gone to visit her mother, like Cassie Halloway thought, but Kyla wasn't the sort to shut her business down and leave during tourist season. The latest disappearance, just last week, was the most suspect of all, because Madge Marquay was a full-time teacher at the high school, and Madelyn's socialite. Her calendar was always filled and she never missed an appointment or a day of work. Until last week. Poor old Henry Marquay was beside himself, and Police Chief Moss Baskerville and his sole officer, Al Gonzales, were poking around in earnest now, with the unwanted help of Madge's friends. Yesterday a small flock of blue-haired Miss Marples had shown up on Tom's doorstep armed with notepads and pencils, hoping that he might supply some clues.

Flocks of old ladies, flocks of sheep, of UFO nuts, religious fanatics, and even tourists who wanted to see UFOs instead of Wild West shows were all conspiring, it seemed, to upset this peaceful, happy existence.

A plume of dust rose to the east, where Thunder Road narrowed into a twisted rut of a one-lane trail as it entered Spirit Canyon. A second or two later, a vehicle emerged, moving toward him at high speed.

Curious, he paused at the intersection of Thunder Road and Old Madelyn Highway. A moment later, he saw that it was a military jeep, an open CJ-5, and as it slowed to turn south on Old Madelyn, the three uniforms gave him a good once over. The two in front were grunts in cammies; in the rear sat a glowering beetle-browed officer dressed to show off his lettuce. Air Force, most likely.

Military types were nothing new to Madelyn: You

had Edwards Air Force Base to the west, China Lake and the defunct Fort Irwin due north, and Twenty-Nine Palms to the southeast, among others, and if it wasn't convoys tooling down Interstate 15, it was jets booming overhead. And every now and then you got soldiers in jeeps sniffing around the hills and canyons behind Madelyn. Tom wondered if they were there for the UFOs, the mutilations, or just to instill a little more paranoia in the locals.

He dismissed the uniforms when he noticed something out of place. It lay on the ground across rutted Old Madelyn Highway, not far from Fort Madelyn, the park's newly restored Union outpost. "What the hell?" he asked aloud, squinting at the mound. It was probably just a big white garbage bag tossed by some thoughtless tourist, but he thought it looked a little like an animal. He crossed the road in five long-legged strides.

"Sweet Jesus." It really was an animal, a white goat, and it lay with its limbs broken and twisted, its head flattened and mushy-looking in the lengthening afternoon shadows cast by the fort wall. "Damn," he whispered as he kneeled and saw the silver choke chain around its neck. It was one of Cassie Halloway's pets. "Damn. Why the hell did I have to be the one to find this?"

Standing again, he saw an unnatural number of stones and rocks scattered around the corpse. One sharp chunk of quartzite was half-buried in the animal's belly. Sadly he shook his head, sick to his stomach. That a human being could do something so cruel to an animal was beyond his comprehension. This was worse than the mutilations: This poor creature had suffered horribly.

Purposefully he trudged back to Old Madelyn Highway, turned south, and walked the hundred yards or so to Cassie Halloway's place. As he approached the driveway, he saw something that tied his gut into an even tighter knot: The numerals "666" had been painted in red across the side of her aluminum mailbox. Gingerly he touched the paint. Dry. It had to have been there awhile, but he hadn't noticed it on the way up. Checking, he saw that the numbers were only painted on the north side of the box. No one coming up from town would notice it.

Wondering how long the numbers had been there, he walked down the dirt driveway to Cassie's neat yellow bungalow. As he ascended the steps onto the shady front porch, he could hear Popeye cartoons playing inside. He knocked. "Cassie? It's Tom."

He heard feet running, then the front door flew open. Giggling, little Eve Halloway grabbed one of his fingers and pulled him inside. "Mama, Tom's here!" she squealed, tugging him down onto the couch in front of the television.

"Be right there, Tom," Cassie called from somewhere deeper in the house.

"Mama's in the bathroom," Eve told him.

"My Lord," Tom said quickly, "that Popeye's one strong fella, isn't he? Wish I could tie a bull's horns in knots like that."

A wispy, deceptively frail-looking child, Eve stared at him with those astoundingly huge dark gray eyes of hers. The six-year-old bore little resemblance to her redheaded mama, and since Cassie wouldn't reveal the father's identity, some of the more rabid Space Friends were convinced that a space alien was her other parent, what with those big eyes and all. Tom, however, was 98 percent sure that police chief Moss Baskerville, who not only had steel-colored eyes, but quite a bit of blond left on his big graying head, was her daddy. Especially since that's what Eve called him. Moss and Cassie had been keeping company for a decade, and you could find him here just about as often as at his little house in New Madelyn, but for some reason, you weren't supposed to mention it.

"Mama got a new tattoo," Eve announced, plunking down beside him.

"Did she now?"

Eve nodded soberly. "Uh-huh. Know what it is?"

"Let's see." Tom removed his hat and scratched his head. "A big old elephant?"

"Huh-uh."

"Oh, well then, I guess it's a can of spinach."

Hands on her hips, Eve suppressed a giggle. "No silly. It's sixes."

"Sixes?" he asked, a fresh set of goose bumps rising.

"Hey, Tom!" Cassie entered, dressed in jeans and sleeveless T-shirt that showed off her pictures. She patted the pink towel turbaned around her hair. "Sorry to keep you waiting. We were putting the finishing touches on the backgrounds for the new play today, and I had a little run-in with a can of paint."

She was proud of the Langtry Theater. It not only paid for the Halloways' modest needs, but in transforming the shabby building at the northern edge of Madland into a saloon-style vaudeville playhouse five years ago, she had transformed herself from itinerant go-go dancer to respectable businesswoman. "I was starting to think I'd never get that stuff out of my hair."

"Mama's hair was purple!" Eve giggled.

"How did you—" began Tom.

"Walked under a ladder. Guess that old superstition has some merit after all." she grinned. "So, Tom, did Evie tell you I got a new tattoo?"

"She said it's a battleship," Tom said somberly.

"Did not! He's fibbing, Mama!"

Tom stood up. "There's no foolin' that girl."

All of Cassie's tattoos were basically the same. The first dated back to the late sixties and was, true to the times, a set of three psychedelic paisleys above her left breast, sort of like the ones Goldie Hawn had on the old "Laugh-In" show. Cass didn't actually start collecting them until she came to Madland nearly twenty years ago and met Gus Gilliam, retired biker turned tattoo artist. Gus had a copy of the Metropolitan Museum of Art book, a real talent with the needles, and he soon convinced Cassie to let him balance out the psychedelic paisleys with a new trio on her right breast. He did them Grandma Moses-style, with tiny American primitive pictures of the seasons within the teardrop shapes. Cassie was hooked. He went on to do a set of Renoirs, Brueghels, and Remingtons before he died.

Fortunately, Gus Junior had inherited his father's gift and his interest, and he took up when his dad left off. Cassie's back, torso, upper arms, and thighs were now a living tribute to the masters. Gus Junior had been on an impressionist kick lately, and Tom wasn't much for them. He favored the Remingtons.

Cassie turned her left arm to expose the inner flesh just above the wrist. "Aren't they gorgeous?"

"They sure are." These were done in a new style and were the first art to appear south of Cassie's elbow.

"They're art nouveau, Aubrey Beardsley," Cassie told him. "Gus outdid himself, don't you think?"

"The colors remind me of Carlo's little Tiffany lamp."

She nodded, pleased. "Same era."

"Look at the detail on that dragonfly wing," he marveled.

"See the little fairy dancing on the flower? Isn't she lovely?"

"She sure is." He hesitated. "Cassie . . ."

"What's on your mind, Tom?" Cassie lowered her arm.

"Need to talk to you about something," he said reluctantly.

"There's coffee on in the kitchen."

"Sounds good."

As they settled at the dinette table, Eve skipped in. "What're you doing?"

"Honey," began Cassie, "why don't you go outside and—"

She silenced as Tom shook his head no. Watching him, she said, "Go watch some more cartoons while Tom and I talk."

"I want to talk too."

"No, Eve."

"But I want—"

"Okay," Tom interrupted. "We're gonna be swapping some recipes. You got some recipes on you?"

"Yuck!" Evie disappeared back into the other room and the TV's volume increased slightly.

Suddenly there was a cracking noise and everything gave a little jerk.

"Earthquake," Eve trilled over the television's chatter. The house creaked and settled in agreement.

Looking at each other, Tom and Cassie waited for another, but it didn't come.

"Been a lot of those little shakers lately," Cassie said.

"Yeah. Hope it means the land's keeping itself settled, not working up to a big one."

"Damned scientists can't make-up their minds. So, Tom, what do you want to talk about?"

"Well, I was just thinking about something Eve said," Tom began. "She called your paisleys 'sixes.'"

"Always has, ever since she learned her numbers. From a distance, they do kind of look like sixes, don't they?"

Tom nodded. "And they're in sets of three."

"Sure. Keeps 'em symmetrical."

"Cassie, somebody painted three sixes on your mailbox."

"What?"

"You know. Six-six-six, like the devil sign. In red. When I saw 'em, they put me in mind of that satanic cult that was around here a couple years back. Six-six-six. They carved the numbers in that gravestone on Boot Hill, then killed a bunch of black chickens—"

"And now somebody's painted some sixes on my mailbox." Cassie sounded unconcerned. "I'm a safe target, so far out of town. You think the cult's back?"

Tom shrugged. "I don't know, but I think maybe it's not random vandalism."

"Shoot, Tom, of course it's random."

"I'd agree with you if Eve hadn't said that about the sixes. Or if . . ." He trailed off, not wanting to tell her the rest.

"Spit it out, Tom."

He stared at her a long moment. "Cass, something else happened. One of your goats is dead."

"That can't be, Tom. they were both there this morning before I took Evie to school." She stood and opened the back door and stepped out onto the stoop. "There's Daisy. Iris? Iris?"

"I found her across the road, by the fort."

Cassie turned to him, her face blanched white. "A car hit her?"

"No, It was done on purpose. Cassie, by the looks of things, I expect she was stoned to death. Moss needs to go take a look."

Cassie sat down slowly. "Lord, I loved that rotten old goat."

"I know."

"So did Evie."

"I don't think you should let Evie go out by herself until Moss figures out what's going on."

"You think the goat and the mailbox are connected?"

"I believe I do," he admitted, wishing he hadn't been the one to find these things, wishing to be gone from here.

Tears threatened to overflow her eyes and she wiped them roughly away. "Those damned satanists. Somebody oughta stone *them*."

"What about the Apostles?" Tom asked.

"Sure, they can do the stoning."

"No, no. I mean they've been getting awful crazy lately with all their apocalypse talk."

"You think they might have done it?"

"Maybe. You ever hear Sinclair's radio show?"

"No." She stared at him. "Tom Abernathy, I'm surprised you'd listen to such garbage."

"I must confess, I listened once or twice way back when they started the station, just one of curiosity. I thought they were sort of amusing." He paused, considering. "I thought the Apostles were harmless, you know, like Janet Wister and her UFO-worshipping friends. But the other night, I caught the program again. Sinclair was ranting and raving about floods and earthquakes and how the Four Horsemen are gonna ride right down Thunder Road and herald the end of the world."

"Sinclair and his group are full of hot air," Cassie said dully.

"Yeah, they are, but it's self-righteous hot air, plus they've got themselves a time frame. They may be up to something."

Raising her eyebrows, Cassie said, "Let me guess. The end of the world will come with the eclipse on Sunday, right?"

"Right you are. Sinclair claims he's been charged with some holy mission to destroy sinners for God. He says the Apostles are the chosen ones."

"Most religions claim that privilege."

Tom nodded. "True, but not like the Apostles, at least to hear Sinclair tell it. Calls himself a prophet. Seems to believe it. When he broadcasts those sermons, you can hear the converts in the background hallelujahing everything he says. They're real riled up. They're zealots, and zealots worry me."

"Well, they have been annoying the tourists," Cassie allowed. "Moss's had to run 'em out of Madland every weekend lately."

"I was thinking about that," Tom said.

"But still, they're a regular Christian religion."

"I don't know, Cass. When Sinclair talks, they're always 'the Prophet's Apostles,' never 'Christians.'"

"Their crucifix is pretty weird, I'll give you that. That big old lit-up cross on top of their church puts me in mind of Las Vegas."

Tom nodded. "You ever notice how they have it rigged?"

"Yeah, It disappears on Sunday morning and shows up again late at night."

"Must use it to gussy up their services. Pretty strange, if you ask me."

"Still, they worship God, not the devil, and I just can't see them killing a poor defenseless animal."

"Maybe," Tom said. "Christians used to sacrifice them all the time and, well, hell, they're still doing ritual cannibalism."

"What?"

"Communion. Christ's body and blood. Thursday night, after the barbecue, maybe we'll give it a listen, see what everyone else thinks. You're coming, aren'tcha?"

"I don't know if I'm gonna feel like socializing, Tom. Moss'll be there if he can, though." She shook her head. "Wish he'd get around to hiring a new man, what with all that's been going on."

"Cass, you can't miss Thursday night." Over the years, dropping in at Tom's on Thursday evenings had become a habit set in stone. "I don't think you should be out here all by your lonesome, anyhow. Especially with this six-six-six business."

"I'll think about it, but don't play daddy, Tom. It's unbecoming."

"How come it's okay for you women to tell us men to be careful, but we get our heads taken off if we say it to you?"

"Changing times." She grinned. "We gotta be as chauvinistic and obstinate as you boys were and make sure you all *know* we don't need you."

"Why, that's just silly."

"Yeah, I know, but it's the way things work. Bunch of fanatics on one side, bunch on the other, have to fight it out. Finally they find a middle ground." She smiled. "As for us women, as soon as we know we've convinced you we can take care of ourselves, why, then I guess we can all tell each other to be careful."

"Women don't make sense," Tom said, shaking his head.

"Men don't either." Cassie gave him a wink. "That's one of the things I like about them."

"You got a point." Tom reached behind him and snagged the phone receiver from the wall. "We need to let Moss know what's going on."

"Fine, but don't you put any of that stuff about paisleys looking like sixes in his mind. If you do, that man'll be breathing down my neck every minute."

"I thought you liked him breathing down your neck," he chided gently.

"Don't start, Tom."

"Yes, ma'am." He left a message for Baskerville,

then took his leave, carefully refraining from telling Cassie to be careful. Instead, he put his Stetson back on and said, "Hope we see you Thursday."

"Tom?"

Hand on the doorknob, he turned and raised his eyebrows.

"What do you think happened to Madge Marquay?" she asked, a tentative tone in her voice.

Once more, those damned goose bumps did a little dance. He stared solemnly at Cass. "Nothing, I hope. Maybe she and Henry had a spat and she took off, and maybe Henry is too embarrassed to say so." He knew that she knew he was spouting bullshit. "What does Moss think?"

She shook her head, her customary bravado gone. "He thinks it's bad. Real bad."

"What about Kyla and Joe?"

"Joe, well, he doesn't know about him, but he's afraid whatever got Madge got Kyla. He's out of leads. None of her friends or relatives have heard from her." Cassie paused. "He's worried, Tom."

"I don't envy his job." He turned the knob and pushed the door open, anxious to be on his way. "I'm sorry, Cass, I've got a four o'clock show."

"You get going, Tom," she said softly, a little too much understanding in her eyes. "We'll see you later."

Outside, he glanced at his watch, then began working briskly down the road toward the Madland entrance. Because of the goat, he'd have to ride one of the horses to the stunt riders' corral instead of stopping by the ranch to fetch Belle, who knew his every move. He felt a surge of annoyance, followed by one of guilt. "Abernathy," he muttered as he crossed the road and walked up the wide rock-lined path to the park's entrance, "it's your own damn fault. You don't want to get involved, you shouldn't be so damned curious."

ABOUT THE AUTHOR

Tamara Thorne lives with her family in California. She is the author of nine horror novels published by Pinnacle Books. Her next novel will be published in July 2004. Tamara loves hearing from readers and you may write to her c/o Pinnacle Books. Please include a self-addressed stamped postcard if you wish a response. Or you can visit her Web site at www.tamarathorne.com.

SINK YOUR TEETH INTO
THESE VAMPIRE ROMANCES
FROM SHANNON DRAKE